MW01241571

Cattle Valley

Carol Lynne delivers another exceptional romance...
PHYSICAL THERAPY is a beautiful story about
redemption and the chance to find where you truly
belong. As always, I am looking forward to her next
wonderful tale. ~ *NovelTalk*

Carol Lynne shines once again. She leaves a brand on
her romance that marks it as hot, emotional, and
sexy. OUT OF THE SHADOW is an exceptional story
about grabbing life by the horns and letting it take
you along for the ride. There is just something about
Cattle Valley that has me eagerly anticipating the
next instalment in this fabulous series. ~ *NovelTalk*

Carol Lynne proves that literary gay sex does not
have to be rough to be exciting, and that love is a
universal turn-on. ~ *Author, Lisabet Sarai*

CATTLE VALLEY
Volume Three

Physical Therapy

Out of the Shadow

CAROL LYNNE

Cattle Valley: Volume Three
ISBN # 978-1-907010-80-4
©Copyright Carol Lynne 2009
Cover Art by Anne Cain ©Copyright 2009
Interior text design by Claire Siemaszkiewicz
Total-E-Bound Publishing

PHYSICAL
THERAPY

Dedication

Dedicated to Dr. Chad Neal.
Thanks for your help and insight.

Chapter One

"Jeffries!" the pilot shouted as he jumped on the helicopter.

Shit. Matt rushed to climb into the helo. He gave Chuck the thumbs up as the Blackhawk lifted into the air. As they flew over the outskirts of Baghdad, Matt could feel sweat begin to trickle down his spine under his flack jacket. This was Iraq. It didn't seem to matter that the sun had set hours earlier, or that they were two hundred feet in the air, the temperature still hovered around eighty degrees.

Just ahead he could see the fire burning from the car bomb that had been driven into an Army outpost, the blowing smoke burning his nostrils. From the report they'd received over the radio, they were to expect serious injuries and several casualties.

Matt's stomach knotted. It was something he never got used to. It didn't matter whether he knew the soldiers personally, they were still soldiers, and because of that, his brothers and sisters.

Chuck set the helicopter down with a light touch. Without time to think, they jumped onto the ground running. The next few moments were organised chaos as the wounded were triaged. The soldiers that managed to escape without serious injury helped load those whose lives depended on getting to Sina Hospital in Baghdad.

Within minutes, the Blackhawk was back in the air, Matt trying desperately to save a boy of about twenty. "Come on," he said as he gave the soldier chest compressions.

Next to him his friend Danny worked on a corporal whose leg had been severed by a flying piece of metal.

Blood. There was always so much blood. It's coppery scent, something he'd never forget. "How's your patient?" Danny asked through his headset.

Matt gave a sombre shake to his head. As long as he continued administering chest compressions, he knew the young man would make it to the hospital alive, but the prognosis was grave from that point on. Miracles had been known to happen, however, and Matt hoped for one for this particular private.

A hand gripped his sleeve. Matt's attention swung to the injured soldier to his other side. The man had been unconscious when they'd loaded him, a piece of shrapnel lodged in his neck. They all knew better than to touch it, so they loaded the soldier and started an IV.

"Help me," the guy gasped.

Evidently in the transfer onto the helo, the piece of metal in the soldier's neck had shifted slightly. Blood was arching upward in copious amounts with every breath the man took.

Matt looked around the interior of the Blackhawk. There was no-one available to help the bleeding man. Matt knew if he stopped the chest compressions on the young man he was working on, he'd surely die moments away from the hospital. *Shit.*

This was the worst part of his job. It was like playing God on a daily basis. *How do you live with the guilt of sacrificing one to save another?*

With a deep breath, Matt continued with the compressions. He looked at the bleeding man beside him. "Try to relax. We're almost there."

"Please," the bleeding man begged.

"I'm sorry," Matt said. "I can't do anything more, you need a surgeon." Even as he said it, Matt watched the private's eyes begin to close. As the Blackhawk touched down, Matt watched the life drain out of the bleeding soldier.

Opening his eyes, Matt sat straight up, a scream still resonating through the room. He rubbed his eyes as he tried to even out his breathing. It was always the same dream, different soldiers, same outcome.

Matt flung back the sweat drenched sheet and swung his legs over the side of the bed. He knew from experience there wouldn't be any more sleep for him. After slipping on a pair of sweats and a T-shirt, he opened the door to his garage apartment, and stepped out onto the small landing.

The night was cool, cold actually, but it was just what he needed. He walked down the stairs to the little courtyard at the back of Isaac's and Sam's house and took a seat on the comfortable chaise.

Trying to push the dream from his mind, Matt focused his attention on his schedule for the coming day. Kyle was making great progress in his therapy, pushing himself harder in each session.

Who could blame the guy? Kyle's desire was to walk down the aisle with his husband-to-be on his wedding day.

A sound from the open window above him drew Matt's attention. There, silhouetted in the moonlight, stood Isaac. Damn. He'd been busted. It wasn't the first time Isaac had caught him up and about in the middle of the night. At least this time he was wearing clothes.

A week after he'd started working for the Doctors Browning and Singer, he'd awakened after yet another nightmare. Seeking refuge in the garden, he hadn't bothered putting on anything but a robe.

It had been a Saturday night, and his bosses had gone to Sheridan earlier in the evening to some kind of dinner party. They'd asked him to go, but he felt uncomfortable spending too much time with the couple. It wasn't that he didn't like them, it was just the opposite. His daydreams were filled with visions of the two of them in various states of undress.

Stretched out on the chaise, Matt tried to think of something, anything, to get his mind off the dream. That night, like now, he'd heard a noise coming from the perpetually open window above him.

What started as voices, talking too softly to be understood, quickly turned into moans of pleasure.

Closing his eyes, Matt had pretended he was in the room with them. His hand reaching down to untie his robe, he fisted his erection as the noises grew louder.

"Fuck me, goddammit!" He heard Sam yell.

Matt's available hand went automatically to his long neglected hole. He rimmed the tightly puckered skin with the pads of his fingers as the sounds of flesh meeting flesh echoed in the cool night.

Bringing his hands to his mouth, he spat on both of them. One returned to its place wrapped around his cock, the other smoothed the moisture onto his ass.

As he worked in two fingers, Matt jerked his cock faster, trying to keep up with the sounds coming from above. He was on the edge of bliss when he heard two voices cry out in ecstasy.

The howls of pleasure from the men upstairs, had his hands working at lightning speed. His fingers seeking out the void in himself that so desperately needed to be filled. His mind drifted and he could see himself sandwiched between the two doctors. His climax roared through him, painted his chest with his own seed. He hadn't realised he'd cried out, but when his breathing returned to normal, he saw something that put a hitch in his breathing. Isaac stood above him at the window completely nude. Their eyes locked for what seemed like hours but was actually only a matter of seconds.

Suddenly embarrassed, Matt quickly closed the robe over his sticky chest and retreated back to his apartment above the garage. They'd never spoken of that night and Matt was eternally grateful. It was one thing to have fantasies about ones bosses, but it was completely different to beat off while listening to them fuck.

Shaking off the memory, Matt looked back up at the window. He heard Isaac say something over his shoulder before disappearing back into the darkness.

Turning his attention to the spring flowers visible in the moonlight, Matt tried to figure out what to do. He'd already put out feelers for another place to live. Kyle said he could rent the apartment above the bakery since he'd moved in with Gill, but Matt was holding out for a house. Of course, if things got much worse between himself and his present landlords, he might have to make the sacrifice.

Leaning his head back on the chaise, he couldn't keep his eyes from glancing up once more. To his surprise, it was Sam who now stood looking down on him.

A noise from directly behind him had Matt out of the chair and dropping to the ground. He closed his eyes as he fought the images trying to swallow him whole. Visions of sniper fire and Danny's death. Danny.

A cry rent the air around him. It wasn't until comforting hands began rubbing his back, that Matt realised the cry had come from him. He looked up into Isaac's concerned face.

"You okay?" Isaac asked, as Sam burst through the open French doors.

Matt closed his eyes and nodded. "I'm fine. You startled me."

Isaac helped him sit back up on the chaise and took a seat beside him. "Need to talk about it?" Isaac asked.

"No," Matt answered. "Just one of the many presents I brought home from the war."

God help him, but it took every ounce of self preservation not to lean into Isaac and accept the comfort the man was obviously willing to provide.

He couldn't help but notice the look the two doctors exchanged. Matt hadn't officially been diagnosed with PTSD (Post-Traumatic Stress Disorder), but that was only because he'd refused to see a doctor. Funny, he was now faced with two. Two doctors who were both looking at him with pity in their eyes.

He'd had enough of that to last a lifetime from his family. Standing, Matt tried to act as though he was fine, knowing in reality he was anything but. "I'm gonna try to get in a couple more hours of sleep. Sorry if I startled you," he said as he walked towards the stairs that would lead him to the safety of his apartment.

"Matt," Sam called.

He stopped walking but didn't turn around. He couldn't. The last thing he needed was to see their faces.

"We're here for you when you're ready to talk. If you need anything, anything at all, let us know," Sam said.

Matt nodded and continued to the stairs. *Yeah, he definitely needed his own place.*

* * * *

As Isaac watched Matt's back as it ascended the stairs, his chest tightened further. He felt Sam's arms wrap around him from behind and turned to embrace his lover of over twenty years. "You ready to go back up?" he asked Sam.

Nodding, Sam gave him a quick kiss. They turned and walked hand in hand back into the house. After locking the door, they made their way to the bedroom.

Sliding into bed, Isaac spooned his body against Sam's back in their customary sleeping position. As the minutes ticked by, he could tell Sam was as awake as he was, but neither of them felt like talking.

Never, in all the years they'd been together had he been tempted to cheat. Isaac pulled Sam closer, needing to feel a sense of normalcy. Matt had him so stirred up and confused, they hadn't been getting along very well lately.

Breathing in the lingering citrus smell of Sam's shampoo, Isaac wondered what the future held for them. He loved Sam to the depths of his soul. So why suddenly had he begun having dreams about Matt? Hell, Matt was young enough to be his son. He should've known better than to let Sam hire Matt.

Isaac had felt that special spark the first time they'd shook hands on Matt's first day on the job. He'd only felt that spark once before, and that was with the gorgeous, loving man in his arms.

"You worried about Matt?" Sam's voice startled him.

He couldn't tell his lover he was thinking about Matt, but not in the way Sam thought. "Yeah," he finally said.

"We should get him to go see Ben Zook."

Isaac's hand moved down from Sam's stomach to brush across the soft hair that surrounded his cock.

"Maybe, but I don't think he's ready to admit to having a problem."

He ran his fingertips over Sam's half-hard erection. It had been over two weeks since the two of them had made love. Lately, they were doing good if they shared the same bed. They didn't have yelling-name-calling fights, but for them, to not be in each others pocket was the same as fighting.

Sam scooted over enough to roll half-way onto his back. The new position still gave Isaac's hands plenty of room to play, while allowing them the ability to reach each other's lips.

"I love you," Isaac said, looking into Sam's light blue eyes.

"You're my world," Sam replied, taking Isaac's length into his hand.

The kisses were natural, comfortable, as they slowly brought each other to completion, pumping their seed onto each other's hands and stomachs.

Afterward, they kissed some more, neither of them in a hurry to clean up. Isaac glanced at the clock. It was two hours before they needed to be up to start their day. Two hours that he knew he'd probably dream about Matt. Two hours of being ashamed of himself.

Chapter Two

Parking in his designated spot, Matt sat in his six-year old Toyota Camry and stared at the employee entrance. It was his first day in his new digs at the clinic. He'd been working out of a room at The Gym while the Doctors had a local contractor, Hal Kuckleman, add a therapy space and small office for him.

He was torn. Part of him had dreaded seeing Isaac and Sam on a daily basis, while the other half was jumping up and down like a kid on the last day of school.

You can do this. Just keep it professional. With new resolve, Matt got out of the car and headed for the door. He removed the security card from his shirt pocket and inserted it into the slot. With the green light flashing, Matt stepped inside.

He'd been to the clinic several times, but usually it was to drop off and pick up patient files. Matt hoped he could get down the hall and to his office before running into Isaac or Sam.

It had been almost three weeks since his meltdown in front of both men. Since then, Isaac had tried on several occasions to schedule an appointment with Ben Zook, the town shrink.

Matt chuckled to himself. What would a guy in Wyoming know about PTSD? He shook his head as he inserted the key into the lock of his new office. Opening the door, he was met by the fresh smell of paint and two gorgeous doctors leaning against his desk.

"Ta-da," Sam said, arms spreading wide.

The light blue walls set off Sam's eyes to perfection. He knew he could easily get lost in them. Matt took an involuntary step towards Sam.

"What do you think?" Isaac asked.

The question stopped Matt in his tracks. *Shit. So much for his resolve to act professionally.* He turned to face Isaac. "It looks great," he said, noticing the way the light blue paint set off Isaac's black hair and tanned complexion. *Oh, hell, he was in trouble.*

The Doctors parted like the Red Sea and gestured to the large wooden desk. "It's beautiful," he said in awe. The desk looked to be antique mahogany with carved legs. Matt thought it was the most gorgeous desk he'd ever seen.

"It's our office-warming, slash welcome-to-the-practice gift," Sam said.

Matt shook his head. "I don't know what to say."

"A thanks is good enough for us," Isaac chimed in.

"Thanks. Uh. Wow." He walked around Sam and sat down in the high-backed leather office chair. He couldn't help comparing this office to the tiny broom closet he'd used in Denver.

Running his hands across the shiny surface, Matt looked at Isaac. "Where did you find it?"

"We didn't," Isaac said. "Ryan Bronwyn from the antique store found it for us. We just told him we wanted something special."

"Well, he certainly delivered," Matt said with a grin. He still couldn't get over the fact these two men had given him such a generous and expensive gift.

Sam put a hand on Matt's shoulder and squeezed just the slightest bit. "Ryan said to tell you that he can get the matching credenza if you're interested."

Matt was so shocked by the intimate touch he heard nothing that came out of Sam's mouth. He saw his lips moving, but all he could think about was having that skilled hand travel its way down his chest to cover his cock. Fuck, the thought had his cock hardening.

He tried to casually cover his growing erection. "Um, I'm sorry, what did you say?" he asked Sam.

"Ryan has the matching credenza if you're interested," Sam repeated.

"Okay," Matt said with a nod. "I'll have to drop in and check it out."

He swung his gaze to Isaac and was surprised to find Isaac's eyes on the hard ridge of his cock trapped behind his khaki slacks. Suddenly worried that Sam would spot the indiscretion, Matt stood.

"I think I'd like to check out the therapy facilities next."

Isaac blinked and turned a beautiful shade of red. He seemed to know that Matt caught him looking. If only Isaac knew that Matt wanted him to do more than look.

* * * *

As Matt checked out each piece of equipment, Isaac secretly checked out Matt. He was a little ashamed at himself, but he didn't have an appointment for another half-hour and Sam wasn't around to catch him ogling.

Examining the back corner of the room, Matt turned and looked at him. "Free weights?"

Isaac grinned and walked towards the gorgeous younger man. "I hope you don't mind, but Sam and I thought it would be nice to have an occasional workout of our own."

Matt shook his head. "I don't mind at all. I spent two years lifting with nothing but free weights."

"Looks like you did a lot of it," Isaac commented. As soon as it was out of his mouth he wished he could pull it back inside.

"Thanks." Matt took a couple of steps until he stood toe to toe with Isaac.

The two men looked into each other's eyes. Isaac could feel the sexual current spark between them. As he started to lean in, zeroing in on those perfect lips, Maggie's voice came over the loud speaker.

"Dr. Singer, you're needed in the emergency room."

Isaac wasn't sure if he was thankful for the interruption or not. He stared into Matt's green eyes for another moment. "I'd better get going."

"Yeah, probably so," Matt replied, licking his lips.

It was all Isaac could do to stifle his groan as the point of that pretty pink tongue was exposed.

"Dr. Singer, you're needed in the emergency room."

Isaac took a step back. "Sam and I are grilling later if you're interested."

Matt blinked at the mention of Sam's name. "Uh, no, sorry. I've already got plans."

"Oh, well okay." Isaac pointed towards the door. "I'd better get going before Maggie comes in here and drags me out by my hair."

Matt nodded and finally broke eye contact. "I've got to get changed for my first appointment anyway."

Without another word, Isaac turned on his heels and practically ran from the room. What the hell was wrong with him? He rounded the corner, and knocked right into Sam.

"Hey, where's the fire?" Sam chuckled.

"Emergency room," Isaac said and gave his lover a quick peck on the lips. "Later," he called as he took off again.

Dammit he loved Sam. So what the hell was going on with him and Matt?

* * * *

After work, Matt went by The Gym to work out. He knew it was stupid now that he had his own place to do it, but he had to think of something to keep him from going home.

The last thing he thought he could handle was sitting across a table from Sam and Isaac. The moment earlier in the day with Isaac still had him on edge. It was evident that they both wanted the same thing, and had it not been for the interruption...hell, who knew what might have happened.

Walking into the familiar building, Matt spotted Nate and Rio at the juice bar. "Hey," he greeted as he took a seat beside Nate.

"Uhh, sorry, Matt, but are you lost?" Nate chuckled.

"Naw, I just missed your ugly face," Matt fired back.

"Oh, well that I can understand," Nate said, flashing his perfect movie star smile.

Matt looked at Rio who snorted. "Get over yourself already," Rio said, restocking the glasses.

He couldn't keep from laughing. Rio was like a horn dog panting after Nate night and day. It was one of the reasons he enjoyed hanging out with the two of them. No matter what they argued about, their love for each other was so transparent, no-one could help but to sit back and enjoy the show.

Kind of like Isaac and Sam. Man, he was so screwed.

"Hey, where'd you go?" Nate asked, snapping his fingers in Matt's face.

"Sorry, got a lot on my mind."

"Hmmm." Nate rubbed his chin. "Wouldn't have anything to do with Doctors Browning and Singer, would it?"

Matt's jaw dropped before snapping back shut.

"Yeah, that's what I figured," Nate said.

"Am I that obvious?"

"Only when you're in the same room with them." Nate put his arm around Matt's shoulders. "If it makes you feel any better, I've seen them look at you a time or two as well."

Matt folded his arms on the bar and put his head down. "What am I supposed to do?"

"Well, if I were you…" Nate began.

"Nate! Keep your nose out of Matt's business," Ryan said from behind them.

Turning his head to the side, Matt watched Nate spin around and greet his other lover. After an x-rated kiss, Nate stuck out his bottom lip. "But, Sheriff, he asked for my advice."

Ryan looked at Rio and shook his head. "What are we gonna do with him? He's worse than all the women in this town put together."

Nate reached down and covered Ryan's cock with his hand. "You mean I'm better than all the women in town put together."

Ryan smacked Nate's hand and blushed. "That goes without saying, but watch it, will ya. There are still a few guys working out in here."

Nate spun back around to Matt and rolled his eyes. "So, as I was saying before I was so rudely *interrupted*. I think you should go for it. Lay it all out on the line, and let the cards fall where they may."

Ryan made a sound in his throat and moved around Nate to greet Rio. As the two of them involved themselves with hellos, Matt thought about what Nate had said.

"Just like that? I just walk up to them and tell them I can't stop thinking about them?"

Nate shrugged. "It's what I'd do."

"Liar," Ryan said from behind the bar. "When you were interested in me and Rio, you did nothing of the kind. You sulked around, and then went out and almost got yourself raped being a damn fool."

Nate waved a hand in the air. "Haven't you ever heard of learning from your past mistakes? Damn, Ryan, lighten up."

Nate winked at Matt. "Seriously, I think that's what you should do."

"But how can I? Isaac and Sam have been together forever."

Rio's bulging biceps appeared next to his head, as the big man leaned on the bar. "Okay, now this, I know a little something about. Ryan and I had been together for years before Nate came sashaying into our lives…"

"I do not sashay," Nate interrupted.

"Yeah, baby, you do. Anyway, I was driving myself crazy because as much as I loved Ryan, I started developing feelings for Nate."

"So what did you do?" Matt asked, sitting up.

"I did nothing. I was afraid of losing what I had with Ryan, so I almost let Nate get away. It was one of the dumbest mistakes I almost ever made. I can't imagine my life without Mr. Nosy Pants." Rio looked over at Ryan. "Can you?"

"Nope. I don't even want to think about it," Ryan said, shaking his head. Matt could see that Nate was hanging on Ryan's every word. Damn they were cute together.

Maybe they were right. After all, who would know more about the topic than these three? "Thanks, guys. I think I'll head on home. Isaac and Sam invited me to grill out with them. Perhaps I should drop in."

"That's the spirit," Nate said. He gave Matt's back a few good slaps and jumped off the stool. "Okay, men, my work here is done. Take me home and ravish me."

Matt was still laughing when he got into his car. He drove back to the house and parked to the side of the garage.

Getting out of the car, he headed to the backyard. When he rounded the corner of the house, Matt stopped short. The two men were sitting at the table just staring at each other, and it didn't appear to be out of lust. Nope, it looked like they were fighting again.

The last thing Matt wanted was to come between them. He quickly turned and started up the stairs.

"Matt? Is that you?" Sam called out.

Shit. Busted. "Yeah."

"Why don't you come on down and have some dinner?"

"Um, I'm not feeling well. I think I'm gonna go lie down, maybe just turn in early."

Within seconds, both Isaac and Sam appeared at the foot of the steps. "What's wrong?" Isaac asked.

"I've got a headache. I think I'm just tired." This was true, so he wasn't technically lying to them.

Sam took the few steps up to stand on the riser beside him. He put his hands on either side of Matt's head and tilted it down to look into his eyes, assessing his condition, Matt supposed.

"You're not sleeping," Sam said.

Being this close to the good doctor, Matt's breathing began to pick up. He tried to tamp down his arousal, but it was just too much, Sam was too close.

The man's eyes broke contact, and began to wander down Matt's body.

Matt gulped as he felt the heat of Sam's gaze on his erection. Looking back up at Matt before turning to look down the stairs at Isaac, Sam nodded. "I think you were right."

Chapter Three

Oh shit. "Wh...what is Isaac right about?" Matt asked. Had they figured out he was attracted to them? Would they fire him?

Sam took his hand. "Can you come down and talk? I'll get you a couple of Tylenols?"

Matt looked down the stairs at Isaac. Had he told Sam what had happened earlier? He closed his eyes. He needed to think. A tug to his hand had him opening them again.

"Come on," Sam coaxed, and led Matt down the stairs.

He watched as Isaac turned and walked to the patio. As Sam led him around the corner, Matt saw the French doors standing wide open. *Inside?* They were doing this in the house, away from witnesses?

Matt started to drag his feet. "Look, Sam, I'm sorry. I couldn't help it," he started.

Sam stopped in front of him and turned around. He placed a gentle kiss on Matt's chin. "Relax."

A kiss. Okay, he got a kiss. That probably meant they weren't going to kick his ass or fire him. As a matter of fact, maybe this talk was a good thing. He gave a slight grin and followed Sam into the house.

Sam led him into the informal den and gestured to the couch. "I'll get you those pills," he said as he turned to walk out of the room.

Isaac must have passed him in the hall, because seconds later he came into the den carrying a bottle of red wine and three glasses. "I thought we might need a drink," he said.

Matt nodded. He knew he could use something a little stronger, but he also knew the Doctors didn't drink much. He seriously doubted if they had any Jack Daniels in the house.

He watched as Isaac poured the wine. He had to know what he was up against before Sam came back into the room. "Did you tell Sam what happened earlier, in the therapy room?"

Sitting beside him on the L-shaped leather sofa, Isaac handed him a glass. "Yes." Isaac looked into his eyes as he took a sip of his wine. "I couldn't lie to him anymore. I hope you'll understand."

Matt didn't get a chance to reply before Sam came back into the room carrying a bottle of water and a bottle of Tylenol. "Thanks," Matt said.

As he opened the bottle and shook out three pills, Sam sat on the other side of him, and picked his wine glass up from the table. Surrounded by heat, Matt felt sweat pop out on his forehead.

He barely managed to get the pills down around the newly formed lump in his throat, but he finally managed it and set the water and pill bottle on the table.

Sam picked up Matt's wine glass and handed it to him. "We seem to have a problem," Sam began.

Matt's eyes flicked to Isaac. "I'm sorry," Matt said automatically.

"Don't be. I'm not," Sam continued. "Since the first day we met you, it seems we've both been attracted to you," Sam said, gesturing between himself and Isaac. "We've held it in because of our love for each other, but it was always there. I'm sorry to say it started to drive a wedge between us. We're not used to keeping secrets from each other. We've been together a very long time."

Isaac took over. Matt's head swung towards the black-haired man. "After what I saw out the bedroom window shortly after you moved in, I thought maybe you were attracted to me, or us, but I wasn't positive. However, my suspicions were confirmed earlier in the therapy room."

Matt quickly gulped his wine, holding the glass out to Isaac. "Can I have some more?" This was too much. It was one thing to lust after ones bosses, but quite another to find out they felt the same.

Isaac refilled Matt's glass. "I came clean with Sam over dinner. I told him I was ashamed of myself, but that I couldn't stop thinking about you, dreaming about you." Isaac reached across Matt and took Sam's hand. "He admitted to having similar thoughts and feelings."

"So why were the two of you obviously fighting when I got home?" Matt asked.

"Because I wanted to talk to you," Isaac answered.

"And I didn't," Sam interrupted. "Even though I've seen you watch me a time or two, I was never given a clear sign of your desire. I was afraid of losing Isaac to you and being left out."

Matt shook his head and set his wine glass on the table. Turning towards Sam, he shook his head and cupped the older man's cheek. "I've been fantasising about both of you, not one over the other, both at the same time. I was ashamed of myself because I know the two of you have been together a long time. I just couldn't stop…"

That was as far as he got before Sam's lips descended on his. At first the kiss was soft, almost shy. When Matt felt Sam's tongue on his lips, he opened immediately. At the first taste of Sam, Matt groaned, and took the kiss even deeper, tongue fucking the older man's mouth.

A groan from beside him had Matt pulling back. Isaac placed his fingers under Matt's chin and turned his head. Now it was Isaac's turn. The two of them didn't start slowly as it didn't seem to be Isaac's way. The kiss was carnal and mind-blowing.

Isaac leaned back on the sofa and pulled Matt down with him. "I want you," Isaac whispered.

Shit. Isaac got straight to the heart of the matter. Matt looked over his shoulder at the other man sitting beside him. He wasn't sure if he wanted to ask Sam's permission or just to join in. Sam must've picked up on his thoughts, because he reached out and started rubbing his hand up and down Matt's spine.

"Are you interested in making a go of this thing between the three of us?" Sam asked, his hand landing on Matt's ass.

"What if it doesn't work?" Matt spoke his fear. "What if one of you gets jealous that the other is spending too much time with me? I don't think I could live with myself knowing I broke up one of the most loving couples I've ever known."

In answer, Sam stood and held out his hand. "Let's go upstairs. We can work things out in a more comfortable environment."

Matt let Sam pull him to his feet. Hell, he knew he'd let these two men do damn near anything they wanted to him.

"Shall I bring the wine?" Isaac asked, getting to his feet.

"No," Sam said. "I think we need to have all our faculties intact for this."

Isaac nodded and wrapped his arm around Matt. The three of them walked up the wide staircase to the over-sized Master bedroom.

Once in their inner sanctum, Matt watched as the two men started to undress. Damn, for being twice his age, both men evidently took very good care of their bodies. He almost drooled when Isaac removed his shirt, revealing a cut six-pack and large, dark brown nipples.

"Are you going to join us?" Sam asked, stepping out of his pants.

"Uh, wow. I'm so busy looking, I don't think I want to take my eyes of the pair off you," Matt said, his voice going deeper.

"No problem," Sam said. He walked over to Matt, fully naked, and began to unfasten his khakis.

Matt felt Isaac's body press against him from the back. Matt automatically leaned back against the wall of Isaac's chest. Warm hands worked their way down Matt's chest to slip under his sports shirt.

The feel of Isaac's fingers tracing his belly button had his cock jerking. Matt looked down as his pants and his underwear were lowered to the floor, his cock springing free to slap against his abdomen. He stepped out of the clothes as Isaac pulled his shirt up and off, flinging it to the chair in the corner.

It was like a dual assault, one he didn't know if he'd survive. Sam began licking Matt's balls before moving up the length of the throbbing erection. "Yeah," Matt groaned as Sam swallowed his cock.

Isaac's fingers continued to map Matt's torso. When those capable hands landed on his chest, Isaac groaned. "Damn, baby, you've got the biggest pecs I've ever felt."

Matt grinned. He'd worked hard developing them. He was glad they were finally being appreciated.

With Sam devouring his cock, and Isaac pinching and rubbing his nipples, Matt knew he wouldn't last. "You guys keep it up and I'm gonna blow."

One of Isaac's hands moved up from Matt's chest to his mouth. "Get me wet," Isaac whispered in his ear.

Matt greedily laved Isaac's fingers, knowing exactly what his new lover was going to do with them. Isaac used his fingers to pull Matt's head to the side. Removing the wet digits, Isaac replaced them with his tongue.

Matt groaned as Isaac spread his ass and tapped against his hole several times before pushing inside. Matt thought he'd died and gone to heaven. He began moving back and forth between Sam's mouth and Isaac's hand.

All too soon, he felt his cum working its way up from his balls. He tried to warn Sam, but Isaac's tongue was still assaulting his mouth. With a warning grunt, Matt's seed exploded from the head of his cock down Sam's throat. At the same time, Isaac went from one finger directly to three.

The bite of pain seemed to enhance Matt's orgasm even more, as he continued to pump streams of cum into Sam's mouth.

After thoroughly cleaning Matt's cock, Sam pulled off and stood. He pressed his chest against Matt's. Reaching down, Matt took Sam's average-sized cock in his hand.

"Yessss," Sam hissed. Matt tore his mouth away from Isaac's to kiss his other lover.

Meanwhile, three fingers deep inside Matt's ass, Isaac started to growl. "Want in." Isaac's fingers disappeared first and then the warmth of his body.

Mourning the loss, Matt turned to look at Isaac. He was standing in the centre of the room with his head down and his hands on his hips. "What?" Matt asked Isaac.

"Condom. We don't have any fucking condoms," Isaac said.

"My wallet," Matt said, turning back to nip at Sam's lips. Manoeuvring Sam over to the bed, Matt had him sit down, his lover's back against the headboard. He heard Isaac toss the khaki pants back onto the floor, and seconds later, he heard the top of the lube bottle pop open.

Crawling between Sam's spread thighs, Matt ran his tongue up the length of his lover's cock. "Don't tease me," Sam moaned.

He felt Isaac's lubed fingers invade his hole once more, and Matt slipped his lips over the mushroom-shaped head in front of him. He swirled his tongue around the prominent ridge, wondering if he'd ever tasted anything so good. Sam's pre-cum was sweeter than any he'd ever had.

Matt thrust his ass back against Isaac's hand, letting him know he was ready. He smiled around Sam's cock as the fingers disappeared to be replaced by the head of Isaac's erection.

Expecting a slow invasion, Matt was surprised when Isaac pushed deep with one agonising thrust. "Fuck," Matt said around Sam's cock.

Sam started chuckling. "Oh, did I forget to mention that Isaac likes his sex rough?"

Rough was fine with Matt, especially after his body became accustomed to the over-sized cock, but it would've been nice to have gotten a little warning.

Sam started fucking Matt's mouth to the pace Isaac had set in and out of his ass. Matt stopped trying to keep up with the horny pair and just enjoyed the ride. He still couldn't believe what had taken place in the span of sixty minutes. Surely he was dreaming.

Isaac's fat cock pegged his prostate and Matt knew he couldn't be dreaming as his cock hardened once more.

"Damn, I love this ass," Isaac panted as he changed angles.

"Gonna," shouted Sam.

"Wait for me," Isaac grunted.

Within the span of seconds, Matt's mouth and throat were being blasted with cum, as Isaac buried himself as deep as possible and came. The dual sensation, combined with his hand that had somehow worked its way to his cock, had Matt joining in as all three slipped over the edge into bliss.

Collapsing in a pile, Isaac quickly tied off the condom and tossed it into the trash can beside the bed. The three of them moved like they'd been doing it for years, Sam in the centre with Matt and Isaac on either side.

They shared kisses, and words of praise. Matt didn't know if he'd ever been so happy. He was still worried about coming between his two lovers, but Sam's next words helped put him at ease.

"I probably should've also mentioned that Isaac's a fuck machine. I've often worried that I wasn't enough for him."

"Shhh," Isaac said, giving Sam a kiss. "You've always been a fantastic lover."

"Yeah, things have been good, but I know you want it a lot more than I do." Sam turned to look at Matt. "Do you think you can help me keep this man satisfied?"

"I'll sure do my best," Matt said with a grin.

Chapter Four

As soon as the alarm went off, Matt screamed, "Danny!"

Sam's head popped up, and his arms immediately surrounded Matt's nude torso. "Shhh, its okay, Matt. You're okay. Wake up."

He heard Isaac shut off the annoying noise before turning on the small bedside lamp. Sam could see the sheen of tears on Matt's face. He could tell Matt was awake, but he still had yet to open his eyes.

As he watched, the movement behind Matt's lids showed a great deal of eye activity. "Do you know where you are?" Sam asked.

He felt Isaac get out of bed. Seconds later his lover reappeared carrying a wet washcloth. Isaac crawled into bed on the other side of Matt and began to clean his face.

"Matt?" Isaac looked from Matt to Sam.

Sam continued to rub soothing circles into Matt's stomach as they tried to bring their young lover around. He wished to hell Matt would get the help he obviously needed. It was hard enough watching Matt go through it before they became lovers, but now it was heart wrenching.

He decided to call Ben after he got to the office and ask if there was something he and Isaac could do to help Matt. Leaning in, Sam began to kiss his lover's neck. "Come on. Let me see those pretty green eyes of yours."

Matt turned to the side and buried his face in Sam's neck. "God, I'm so embarrassed," Matt said. "My first morning with the two of you and I pull this shit."

"Hey," Isaac said, spooning himself against Matt's back. "No need for embarrassment around us. We're doctors don't forget."

"You guys must think I'm really screwed up."

Sam pulled back enough to tilt Matt's chin up. With Matt finally looking him in the eyes, Sam leaned in and kissed him. He wasn't sure if he was trying to comfort Matt or just take his mind off the nightmare, but the kiss grew in intensity. Before long, Matt's tongue was tickling Sam's tonsils as he started to rub his morning wood along side of Sam's.

Not wanting Isaac to feel left out, Sam reached around Matt to run his hand over his lover's hip. He could feel the muscles of Isaac's ass contract as he began to thrust himself against Matt's ass.

They broke their kiss for some much needed oxygen and Matt pulled Sam even closer, rubbing harder. This time, Sam was the first to cum, his cock exploding in a mind-blowing orgasm.

He heard Isaac's familiar grunt and knew his long-time lover was coming against Matt's ass. Sam looked into Matt's eyes, wondering why he hadn't come and saw the tears again.

He ran his tongue over Matt's lips and gave him a sweet kiss. "Come for me, lover. Forget everything else, and let yourself go."

Two more thrusts and Sam felt Matt's warmth blossom between them as his lover dug his short nails into Sam's back. "Everything's going to be okay," Sam soothed as Matt's breathing returned to normal.

* * * *

"So, this was the last session before the big day on Saturday, you nervous?" Matt asked Kyle.

Kyle grinned. "About the wedding? Hell no. About walking down the aisle? Hell yes."

Matt put a hand on Kyle's shoulder. "You'll do fine. You've worked damn hard to get this far this fast. But, and I stress that word. But, if you start to feel shaky just signal for the chair. No one's going to think any less of you if you can't make it through the whole ceremony."

Kyle pulled Matt into a hug. "Thanks. I couldn't have done this without you."

"Sure you could've. It was just a matter of asking for help."

"Speaking of," Sam's voice came from the doorway.

Matt released Kyle and turned around. "Yes?" he asked.

"Can I talk to you in my office when you're finished?" Sam asked.

"Sure, we're wrapping up here. Give me a few and I'll be in," Matt winked.

Sam smiled and left. Kyle punched Matt in the arm. "You've been holding out on me."

"Ow," Matt laughed and rubbed his arm. "I'm not holding out, okay. Shit, did you have to raise a bruise?"

Kyle laughed and rolled his eyes. "You've got something going with Dr. Browning? What about Doc Singer?"

Matt winced. He didn't want to lie to his new friend, but he didn't think the Doctors wanted the news spread all over town either. "We're trying it, the three of us, but you have to swear to not let that get around."

Kyle's eyebrows rose. "Both? Damn." Kyle whistled.

"Yeah, well, it's brand new, so I don't want to jinx it by saying too much."

"I get ya," Kyle said with a nod. He pointed towards his wheelchair. "Bring me that monster, and I'll get out of your hair so you can go play kissy-face with Dr. Browning."

Matt blushed, but quickly retrieved Kyle's chair. Could that really be what Sam wanted him for? The prospect put a smile on his face.

He got Kyle settled and followed him out the door. "I'll see you on Saturday," he said, waving goodbye to Kyle.

"I'll be the white guy in the tux," Kyle said.

Chuckling, Matt knocked on Sam's door. "Come in."

Matt stepped in. "Shut the door and come here," Sam said.

After doing what he'd been told, Matt walked towards Sam's desk. "You wanted to see me?" he asked.

Sam stood and pulled Matt into his arms, giving him a kiss to remember. When they eventually broke apart, Sam held him a little tighter. "I wanted to talk to you again about going to see Ben Zook."

Matt blinked. *What?* He pushed against Sam's chest as he took a step back. "That's what you called me in here for? So you could use kisses to get me to go see a shrink? A guy I've never even met?" He shook his head. "That's low, man."

He started to walk back towards the door. "Wait," Sam called. "I heard you talking to Kyle. If I remember right, it was something about him getting better once he'd asked for help. Well, take your own advice."

Matt suddenly felt betrayed. He'd listened to this shit from his folks until they'd driven him away. The last thing he needed was for his lover to start in on him. Maybe he needed to rethink the whole situation.

He looked over his shoulder. "What the hell would you know about it? Maybe I deserve the nightmares. Just stay the fuck out of my head."

Matt was so pissed he was shaking. He stopped by the receptionist desk and told her to reschedule his appointments for the rest of the day. With that taken care of, he gathered his briefcase and left the building.

He didn't give it a second thought as he pulled up in front of Brewster's Bar. It may have only been eleven but he was thirsty.

* * * *

"Hey, Holly," Isaac said, walking into the small lab. "Have you got those reports I asked for?"

"Um, just finishing the last one," she said with a grin.

Isaac decided to head off any undue gossip. "We need them for some additional life insurance we're looking in to."

"Uh huh," Holly replied, not looking up from the computer screen. The printer started spitting out several sheets of paper which she neatly put into file folders.

Shit, maybe she isn't buying it. Well, he was the boss, dammit. He shouldn't have to explain himself. He took the folders Holly handed him and thanked her for processing them in a rush.

Walking down the hall, he opened the first folder and took a peek. A wide smile spread across his face and he felt like pumping his arms in the air. Isaac immediately headed towards Matt's office.

When he found the door locked, he asked their receptionist, Jill, about Matt. He was a little surprised when he was informed that he'd left for the day.

Next, he stopped by Sam's office, hoping he wasn't already with a patient. After a brief knock, he stuck his head inside the incredibly tidy office. Sam was sitting at his desk with his head in his hands.

He walked in and shut the door. "Hey, what's up?" he asked, going to sit on the corner of Sam's desk.

"I fucked up," Sam mumbled.

"Huh? You never fuck up. What's going on?" He laid the folders in front of Sam.

Sam's worried eyes scanned them. It was obvious what they were. They'd all taken blood tests that morning.

"Let's just say, I'm not sure we'll need those results for anything," Sam said, rubbing his eyes.

Isaac felt his chest tighten. "You've changed your mind?"

"Not me, but I think maybe Matt has. I brought up Ben Zook again." Sam looked up at Isaac. "He said something that I can't stop thinking about."

"What?" Isaac couldn't take the pained expression on Sam's face and pulled him out of the chair and into his arms.

"He said maybe he deserved the nightmares." Sam sighed and buried his face just under Isaac's chin.

Isaac ran his hands over Sam's back. He needed to think. No, what he needed to do was call Ben. He placed a kiss to Sam's forehead. "Will you trust me enough to let me handle this one?"

Sam looked up at him, his light blue eyes filled with sorrow. "I'm sorry if I screwed things up."

Isaac shook his head. "Don't apologise for trying to help someone who means a lot to us. I think Matt's temper might be a symptom of the problem. Don't take it personally, honey."

He covered Sam's lips with a kiss, heavy on the love, light on the passion. He doubted either of them felt 'in the mood' for anything deeper.

"I'm gonna try and find Matt. Will you be okay?"

Sam nodded. "Call me if you find him."

"I will," he said, giving Sam another kiss.

* * * *

"Tequilla," the man two stools down ordered.

Matt glanced over. Evidently he wasn't the only one who needed the hard stuff this early in the day.

"Thanks," the guy said when the bartender handed him the shot. He downed it in one swallow, and slammed the glass on the bar. "Another with a beer chaser."

The older man caught Matt looking. "What? A guy can't have a drink when he needs one?"

Matt held up his glass of Jack. "Didn't say that at all."

The man chuckled and shook his head as his drinks were placed on the bar. "We're a pair, huh? Barely noon and we're both trying to forget."

"Something like that," Matt said as he tipped his glass back.

"Ahh, you're so young. What could you possibly have to forget?"

Matt bristled at the question. "Age has nothing to do with the amount of bad memories stored up here," he said, tapping his temple.

The guy seemed to think it over. "I suppose you're right." He picked his shot up and held it out to Matt. "Cheers to us."

Matt tapped the man's glass with his own. "Cheers."

The guy downed his shot, and nothing else was said. Matt thought of all the things he wished he could forget. He pulled out the dog tags he still wore around his neck and rubbed his fingers over the thin metal.

"You a service boy?"

Matt said nothing, but gave the man a nod.

"Me, too. Two tours in Vietnam."

That got Matt's attention. His eyes narrowed as he studied the older man. "You don't look old enough."

The guy laughed. "Well, you know what they say about black skin. I'm damn near sixty."

Matt nodded and took another drink.

"You just get back?"

"Yep, going on six months ago."

The guy slid over a stool and held out his hand. "Name's BJ."

Matt shook BJ's hand. "Good to meet you."

"How're you handling things now that you're back in the States?"

Matt just shrugged. The last thing he wanted to do was admit to a stranger in a bar that he felt like he was falling apart most days. That every loud noise made him jump, and every night he saw his best friend killed over and over. Naw, this guy didn't need to hear all that. "As good as can be expected, I guess."

"Well you're lucky then. Hell, they put me in the loony bin for almost a year after I got back."

Matt eyed BJ a little closer. "Is that why you drink?"

BJ looked back. "Maybe. I've had thirty-six years to get over the dreams, but every once in a while, they catch up with me."

Matt's throat seemed to constrict. "So...they don't go away?"

"Never. Not entirely anyway. I've just learned to deal with them. Time helps, don't get me wrong. They happen a lot less frequently nowadays, but I don't let them rule my life anymore. I've also learned it's easier to share them with the person who loves me rather than to go it alone."

45

BJ picked up his beer and drank it in three swallows. "Went through quite a few lovers before I figured that out. Got me a good one now though. We've been together going on twenty years."

Matt finished his drink and slapped some money on the bar. "It was nice to meet you, BJ."

"You ever feel like talking, just ask the bartender. He knows where to find me."

"Thanks." Matt walked out of the bar and stood on the sidewalk. He was surprised to see Isaac sitting on the hood of his car.

"Need a ride?" Isaac asked, not moving from his spot.

Matt wasn't sure what the hell he needed. He knew he couldn't go back to work, not in the condition he was in. He knew he wasn't drunk, but he was well on the way. "Yeah, if you don't mind."

Isaac pushed himself to his feet. "Don't mind at all. We'll have to take your car though. I rode into work with Sam."

Matt nodded and tossed Isaac the keys. His mind kept going back to BJ. The man was almost sixty and still had nightmares occasionally. He also thought about what else BJ had said. Matt wondered if he'd ever be able to open up about memories. Would it make the guilt any less his? He knew it would require a great deal of thinking.

Chapter Five

Sitting straight up in bed, Matt wiped the sweat from his forehead and tried to get his breathing under control. The dreams were coming even more frequently as the days went by.

He looked at the clock. Shit, it was only two. What time had he gone to bed, seven-thirty, eight? He remembered Isaac driving him home, and he remembered telling him he needed to be alone for a while.

Matt threw back the covers and went to take his customary tepid shower to wash off the 'night sweats' as he referred to them. Standing under the cool spray, his dream tried to encroach upon his waking hours. "No!" he yelled.

Drying off, he tried to figure out why the dreams were getting worse. So far he'd relived almost every moment he'd spent with Danny before...

After slipping on his robe, Matt walked out to the tiny living room and sprawled on the second-hand couch. His gaze went to the cheap red photo album. He couldn't figure out why he still had the damn thing. It brought him nothing but grief and guilt.

Matt pushed himself to his feet and walked towards the fridge. Maybe if he ate something he'd be able to go back to sleep.

As he stood at the kitchen window eating a cold slice of pizza, he noticed the lights in the main house were off, but the one at the back door had been left on. He wondered if it was their way of inviting him inside.

He should probably apologise to Sam. Isaac had read Matt the riot act on the way home from Brewster's. He'd done it in a civilised way, but Isaac had definitely made it known that Sam was only concerned because he was becoming emotionally involved.

The worst part about it was Matt knew Isaac had been right. He'd seen the worry in Sam's eyes earlier in Sam's office.

Before he knew it, Matt was on his way down the garage stairs. He tried the back door and smiled when he found it unlocked. Making sure to throw the deadbolt, he walked quietly upstairs.

He leaned against the threshold of the Master bedroom and watched Sam and Isaac. They were spooned together with Isaac nestled against Sam's back. *God they're gorgeous together.*

Letting the robe fall from his shoulders, Matt carefully lifted the covers and slid in. He turned to his side to face Sam and reached across him to hold Isaac's hip.

Matt didn't know how long he watched Sam sleep, the moonlight coming in the window setting Sam's handsome features off to perfection. The longer he studied, the heavier his eyes became, until sleep finally overtook him.

* * * *

In the early morning hours, Sam woke to find Matt curled up against his chest. The tight feeling in his chest loosened a little. He'd been so worried he'd screwed everything up. Isaac had tried to reassure him that he'd done nothing wrong, but he'd pushed and he knew it.

He wasn't intentionally trying to wake Matt, but he needed to make sure he was really there, beside him. When had Matt come to them? Did he have another bad dream?

Sam shifted his head on the pillow until his lips were a hairs breadth from Matt's. "I'm so glad you're here," he whispered, lips brushing over Matt's.

Those green eyes opened, taking the kiss deeper. He felt Matt's tongue press against his lips and eagerly opened for it. His lover swept the interior of Sam's mouth, moaning.

He pulled back just enough to break the kiss and looked into Matt's eyes. "I'm sorry."

Matt shook his head. "No. I'm the one who should apologise. I know you were trying to help. I'm just not very good at accepting it."

He pushed harder against Matt, needing to feel him. He grinned when Isaac's warm body followed, that hard cock sliding across the crack of his ass. "I think we woke Isaac," he whispered.

Matt rose up on his elbow to look over Sam. "Morning," Matt said to Isaac. "I hope you don't mind. The door was unlocked."

"For you," Isaac answered. "Only for you."

Sam ducked his head so Matt could lean over him and share a kiss with Isaac. "You okay?" Isaac asked Matt.

Matt's body tensed under Sam's hands. "No, not really, but I think I need the two of you."

"And we need you," Sam said, rubbing Matt's muscled back. He gave a light smack to Matt's hard ass. "Come on, scoot in here between me and Isaac. Let us both love you."

Sam felt Isaac move back to make room for Matt, who proceeded to crawl over the top of him. Sam groaned as Matt lingered, rubbing against him just a little.

He turned over to face Isaac with Matt safely tucked between them. Sam wasn't about to let the opportunity pass him by as he began to explore each ridge and dip of Matt's well developed torso.

"Feels good," Matt said.

"Let us make you feel better," Isaac said as he started rubbing against Matt's body.

Sam and Isaac both leaned forward and shared a three-way kiss with Matt, all of them moving against each other. He felt his cock glide across Matt's smooth hip as he reached for that sweet long dick. He chuckled to find Isaac's hand already there. Sam decided to move down to Matt's balls as he let Isaac jack Matt off.

Sam licked his way from Matt's lips to his gorgeous pecs. He laved and nipped at the heavily muscled chest as he started grinding his cock against Matt's hip. "Gonna," he moaned without releasing the nipple between his teeth.

"Yeah, together," Isaac panted aloud, doing his own share of grinding.

Within seconds they were all covered in sticky white cum one right after the other. He released Matt's nipple afraid he'd bite the damn thing off as his cock gave its final spurt.

Sam nuzzled against Matt's neck as the three of them began finger painting Matt's chest and stomach. "Nice," Isaac said.

"Mmm hmm," Sam agreed.

Matt rose up on his elbows to look over Sam. "You got a new clock?" Matt asked.

Sam nodded. "This one plays nature sounds to wake you up in the morning." He never again wanted Matt to wake like he'd done the previous day. Never.

Matt didn't say anything, but Sam could tell by the look in Matt's eyes he knew why Sam had done it. Sam pulled his lover's head down for a kiss, threading his fingers through Matt's thick hair.

Isaac started snickering and they broke the kiss to look at him. "What?" Sam asked.

Isaac shook his head. "We definitely need to get into the shower. You've just smeared his head with cum."

Sam withdrew his hand and smiled at Matt. "Sorry."

Matt chuckled. "Don't be. I hear protein's good for the hair."

That got all of them chuckling. "I'd better get up. I need to run by the clinic for a bit before the wedding and check on a few people."

"It's only six," Isaac said. "Stay and take a nap with us."

Sam gave Isaac a deep kiss, tongue sliding in so naturally. "We'll have plenty of time for napping later. If I get my stuff done then I can be lazy with the two of you the rest of the weekend."

Isaac groaned and sat up. "Well, I guess the least we can do is shower and fix you breakfast before you leave." Isaac leaned over and kissed Sam and Matt. "We've never had three in the shower, might be fun." He waggled his brows.

* * * *

Pulling up to the house, Sam grinned. If he knew Isaac, he'd bet his lover still had Matt in bed. He could tell by the way Isaac touched Matt over breakfast that he was hungry for something other than food.

He looked at his watch as he walked towards the house. Gill and Kyle's wedding was in an hour and they needed to get ready and head to the park.

Sam knew it was a big day, not only for the happy couple but for Matt as well. Matt had worked damn hard to get Kyle back on his feet and walking before the ceremony. It was a testament to Matt's skills as a therapist and as a friend. Sam knew all too well that caring about your patients helped tremendously in the healing process.

He let himself inside and looked around at the breakfast dishes still sitting on the table. Yep, things must've happened pretty quickly after he'd left.

Sam stopped to gather clothes as he made his way upstairs. As he walked into the Master bedroom he heard noises and running water coming from the en suite. Dropping the clothes into the dirty clothes hamper, he went in to investigate.

"Fuck this ass feels good," Isaac said.

Without a word, he leaned against the sink and watched his two lovers play. He never thought he'd enjoy seeing Isaac make love to another man. As a matter of fact, he'd often threatened bodily harm if Isaac ever strayed, but this was different. This was Matt, and the two of them together were breathtakingly beautiful.

"Gonna cum so hard you'll taste it, baby," Isaac ground out, voice going deep and scratchy.

He found himself unzipping his pants and reaching inside as he watched. Isaac's long thick cock pounded in and out of Matt's ass, the sound of slapping skin heard over the running water. *God, they're sexy.*

Sam used his own pre-cum to lube his cock as he stroked himself to Isaac's rhythm. He loved listening to Isaac talk dirty. It appeared Matt liked it too. Matt's hand was working his own cock for all it was worth, with his head down. Sam knew what Isaac's cock felt like when he got into such a frenzied pace. He knew Matt was probably having a hard time catching his breath as Isaac continued to assault that sweet spot inside.

"Take it, take my cock."

He assumed by the grunts coming from Matt and the howl Isaac let loose, they'd climaxed. It was their post-coital kiss that pushed Sam over the edge, cum shooting, landing on his favourite shirt. He hadn't realised he'd shouted until the shower door opened and Matt and Isaac were smiling.

"Hey, you, just get home?" Isaac asked.

Matt looked embarrassed as hell to be caught fucking. They'd have to get that straightened out quick. Matt needed to know Sam wasn't jealous of him. Especially with the way Isaac was looking at Sam's cock. Yep, his man still wanted him. After all these years Matt would only enhance their love life, not destroy it.

Without turning off the shower, Isaac held out a wet cloth for Sam. "You might want to clean that off before it stains."

Sam looked down at his cum-soaked shirt and grinned. "Hell it was worth having to buy a new one. That was the hottest thing I've ever witnessed." He looked into Matt's eyes. "I want to watch again sometime."

Matt's eyes told him the message had been received. He quickly dabbed at the white seed on his shirt. "So, did the two of you manage to do anything besides fuck all morning?"

Isaac looked at Matt for a second and shook his head. "No. That's pretty much it. We did snooze for a few, but fuckin' and playing was our main activity."

Although he was sorry he missed it, Sam thought it was probably good that Isaac and Matt had the time alone. He looked at his watch. "You'd better get moving or we'll be late for Kyle's momentous walk down the aisle."

The shower was shut off and Sam pulled a couple of towels off the shelf, handing them over. Isaac threw the towel to the floor and walked right up to Sam, kissing him immediately. "I'd rather dry off on you," he practically growled, sticking his hand down the front of Sam's open pants.

Oh, he loved it when Isaac got like this. He wasn't always able to keep up with his lover, but it felt good to be wanted, and wanted often. He thrust against Isaac's hand. "I'd love nothing more than to crawl back into bed with you, lover, but people are counting on us."

Isaac kissed him. "Later, you're mine."

"I've always been yours," he said, kissing his man.

Chapter Six

Matt got out of the car and looked at the gazebo. It was decorated in flowers and ribbons. People were milling around greeting each other, all in all, a typical wedding. He felt himself start to drift.

"You coming?" Sam yelled as he and Isaac made their way up a slight slope.

Matt nodded and followed in their shadow. It felt like his feet were mired in sand as he slowly trudged up the hill. Sam stopped once more and turned around. "Everything okay?"

"Yeah, I just need a second," Matt answered.

Sam gave him a rather short nod and turned to look up at Isaac. Matt knew what Sam was probably thinking. It wasn't that he didn't want to be seen with the doctors as a couple, he just didn't want to wig out, not here, not now, but he felt it coming. Danny was coming and there would be no stopping him.

At the top of the rise, Sam and Isaac were already shaking hands with a giant of a man he didn't know.

He'd met Wyn briefly and assumed the big guy was his partner Ezra. Nate and his men were there, so at least he knew someone.

Wyn turned to Matt with his arm around his partner. "Matt, this is my better and bigger half, Ezra James. Ezra, this is Matt Jefferies."

"Nice to meet you, Matt," Ezra said. Matt's hand was swallowed in Ezra's. *Damn.*

"And you as well," Matt replied.

"I heard you've been thinking of renting Kyle's apartment? Well, have I got a deal for you. I'm looking to sell my house, but the buyer won't be able to make the sale until the end of summer. I thought maybe you'd be interested in it for a couple of months until you find something more permanent," Wyn said to Matt.

Matt saw Isaac and Sam both stop their discussions and turn towards him. Hell, he didn't know if this thing with Isaac and Sam was going to last a day, a week, or a year.

"Yeah, uh, can I get back to you on that?" he asked.

"Sure, just let me know and I can meet you at the house sometime to show you around."

"You won't find a better offer. Wyn's house is gorgeous," Nate said. Matt was trying to figure out if Nate was playing devil's advocate. Was this his way of pushing them into talking about the future?

Matt nodded. "I've been by it, you're right, Nate, it's a beautiful place."

The music started up in the background, signalling people to take their seats. "Shall we?" Ezra asked Wyn and gestured to the gazebo

"Talk to you guys at the reception," Wyn said as Ezra led him away.

The vibes coming off Isaac and Sam were apparent. He knew they weren't happy with him. He didn't quite understand why though. They hadn't talked about the future. Maybe he was just a passing phase in their long relationship.

Matt pointed to the car pulling up. "That'll be Kyle," he said to Isaac. "I'm going to make sure he's really up for this. If the two of you want to find a seat, I'll join you when I can."

Isaac reached out and brushed his fingers over Matt's hand. He turned his palm up and captured his lover's hand, trying without words to reassure him. Isaac looked at him for several moments before giving him a slight nod. "We'll be off to one of the sides so you can slip in."

"Thank you," he said. He hoped Isaac understood the sentiment was for more than the seat.

He watched as Isaac put his hand to Sam's lower back and led him to the rows of pretty white chairs...pretty white chairs...white chairs. Matt blinked several times and shook his head, trying to get the image from sticking.

Taking a deep calming breath, he headed towards Kyle. "You ready for this?" he asked, bending to whisper in Kyle's ear.

"Hell yeah," Kyle said with a smile.

"I'll make sure you get your footing before I take the chair away," Matt told him.

Kyle reached out and shook his hand. "I'll never be able to thank you enough."

"Just seeing you walk down that aisle will be all the thanks I'll ever need," he said. He didn't know if he'd ever seen anyone so nervous and happy at the same time.

When Gill approached, Matt pushed Kyle's wheelchair into position and waited. As soon as Kyle stood, Matt heard the soft gasps from the guests. Once Gill had a hold on the shaky man, Matt stepped back, taking the chair with him.

As they slowly made their way down the aisle, Matt began to worry that Kyle wouldn't make it standing for the entire ceremony. He wheeled the chair around the outside of the chairs towards the gazebo.

Spotting his lovers, he stopped and whispered in Isaac's ear. "I think I'd better be ready with the chair in case Kyle needs it."

Isaac turned his head to momentarily brush his cheek against Matt's. "Okay, I'll tell Sam," Isaac whispered back.

He positioned the chair off to the side of the proceedings, as the happy couple stood arm in arm. Within moments, their faces changed from Kyle and Gill to him and Danny. Sweat began running down his face as the memories began pouring back.

"You up for a movie?" Matt asked.

Danny looked up at him from his bunk. "I thought maybe you'd want to stay in and work on the album?"

"Again?" he asked, plopping down on the mattress beside Danny. "We just worked on it."

"Yeah, but mom sent a couple of new magazines." Danny held up the thick bridal magazines.

Rolling his eyes, Matt took one and started flipping through it. He'd never met a man so excited by the prospect of a wedding. Danny wanted to plan every second, every flower, and every table arrangement of the ceremony.

"You know, people are gonna start to talk," he teased.

Danny shrugged his shoulders, intent on a picture of a flower arrangement. "Let them." Danny held the picture in front of Matt's face. "What do you think of this flower right here," Danny said, pointing to the page. "It's called Stephanotis. It's supposed to smell really good."

"It's pretty," Matt said, looking at the star-shaped flower. "Kinda small though."

"I know, but it's used as more of an accent flower." Danny studied the picture for a few more seconds and got out his scissors. "I think it'll be nice in the table arrangements. That way our guests can have something pretty to smell as they sit there."

Danny got out his bottle of glue and attached the small picture to the page with the other flowers.

Matt's stomach made a horrible churning noise. "You okay?" Danny asked.

Rubbing his torso, Matt laid back on the narrow bunk. "I think I'm coming down with something. No big deal."

Matt blinked when he heard someone in his ear. "Let's get you home."

He was barely aware of being led down the hill, warmth on each side of him. Before he knew what was happening, he was being put in the back of a car. He looked over at Isaac's concerned face. "What happened?" *Shit, please tell me I didn't freak out in front of everyone.*

Isaac pulled Matt into his arms. "It's okay. You just seemed a little lost, so we thought it would be best to get you out of there."

"Did anyone see?" Matt asked, embarrassment turning his face red.

"I don't think so," Sam answered from the front seat.

They rode back to the house in silence, Isaac rubbing Matt's arm. When they pulled up, Isaac didn't immediately open the door. "Can you talk about it?"

Matt looked at Isaac's concerned face. He remembered what BJ had told him in the bar. "Maybe." He pointed up to his small apartment and handed Isaac his keys. "Can you go up there and get something for me?"

"Sure, baby, anything you want."

"On the bookshelf, or maybe the coffee table, there's a red photo album. Can you bring it to me?" Matt asked as Isaac helped him out of the car.

"I'll get it. Why don't you let Sam take you inside, where you can lie down."

Matt nodded and was passed to Sam's strong embrace. "I've never talked about any of this stuff, so you'll have to be patient."

* * * *

Isaac waited until Sam got Matt inside before going up to his apartment. He stepped inside and looked around the room, finally spotting the album on the couch. Curious, he sat on the sofa and held it for several moments before opening it. He hoped he wasn't breaking Matt's trust, but it was a mystery he was dying to take a peek at.

Flipping through the book, Isaac felt his chest tighten. Every page was filled with collages of wedding pictures, everything from tuxes to mock menus. Was Matt planning a wedding?

He could tell by the dirt and grime on the red cover that the book was old, or maybe it had just been in the desert for too long. He suddenly felt uneasy and closed the album. It was now obvious why Matt had wigged out a little at the wedding.

Isaac tucked the book under his arm and went to deliver it to its rightful owner. Sam must've heard the door close because he called out before Isaac had a chance to head up to the bedroom.

"We're in the media room."

He changed directions and went to the northeast corner of the house. Instead of the reclining media chairs he and Sam usually sat in to watch movies, his lovers were entwined on the big fluffy sectional sofa.

"We thought we'd take a break from life and have ourselves an Indiana Jones marathon."

Sam gave him a look that said Matt wasn't yet ready to talk. "Okay," Isaac placed the book on the bar. "Do you want me to make some popcorn?" he gestured towards their very own popcorn machine.

"Yep, that's why we haven't started the movie yet," Sam chuckled. "You know you're the best at it."

Isaac rolled his eyes and grinned at Matt. "Don't listen to him, baby. He's just too lazy."

While the corn was popping, Isaac opened the small fridge and handed out cans of soda. "I don't suppose you've put the movie in either?"

"I didn't, did you?" Sam asked Matt.

"No, I don't know where you keep them," Matt answered. Isaac knew Sam was right. Matt still seemed a little out of it.

Pulling open the large cabinet, Isaac got out the first couple of Indy movies. By the time he got them in, put the popcorn into bowls and sat down, the previews were over and the movie was starting.

Sam had pulled the big rectangular footstool up to the sofa so it was more like a bed with piles of pillows. He lifted one of the bowls over Matt to Sam. Isaac couldn't help glancing at Matt, who'd barely said a word.

"Want some?" Isaac asked.

Matt took a handful of popcorn and ate it piece by piece. Isaac loved to watch the way different people ate their corn. He grinned at Matt and took a handful of the buttery goodness and stuffed the whole thing into his mouth. Of course a few pieces fell to the couch which had Sam bitching.

"See, Matt, that's what not to do when you're a forty-seven year old man."

Leaning over, Isaac held his buttery hand to Sam's lips. His lover rolled his eyes and made a disgusted sound in his throat, but managed to lick each and every digit. By the time Sam was finished, Isaac's cock was definitely perking up. One look at Matt, however, and Isaac decided to settle in with his men and have some quiet time.

Poor Matt looked like he carried the weight of the world on his shoulders. Isaac set his bowl aside and wrapped his body around the hurting man. "This okay?" he asked.

Matt nodded and rested his head on Isaac's chest. Sam reached over to the basket at the side of the couch and came back with a blanket which he proceeded to spread over the three of them.

Isaac felt Matt's body begin to relax in his arms. If this is what Matt needed him for, he was more than willing to hold the man the rest of his life. The thought surprised him, but he realised he meant it.

They'd have to work on the rest step by step, until Matt trusted them enough to fully open up. Isaac's gaze went to the red album on the bar. It appeared they had a lot to learn about their new lover.

Chapter Seven

Matt opened his eyes. The DVD menu was on the screen attesting to the fact they'd all fallen asleep before the end of the second movie. His eyes travelled the room, coming to rest on the red album, the cause of many of his nightmares.

He managed to wriggle out of the sandwich Isaac and Sam had put him in the middle of, and went to the bar. He picked up the book and ran his hand over the dusty cover. It didn't seem to matter how many times he'd tried to clean the red material, the dust was always there, haunting him.

Leaving the room, Matt took the album to the patio where it was too dark for him to be tempted to look at the pages. He sat in his favourite lounger and clutched the book to his chest. He'd rather have Danny here to hold and tease, but this was the next best thing. Danny had put his heart and soul into every page Matt now held.

He wondered for the millionth time whether it was right that he still had it. Right or not, he decided he wasn't ready to give it up.

"Matt?" Sam's voice sounded from behind him.

"Yeah," he answered.

Sam walked around the chair and looked down at him. "Mind if I join you?"

Matt shook his head and moved his feet, clearing a spot for Sam. "What're you doing out here in the dark?"

"Hiding," Matt said. He wished he could hide from himself at times, but the dark was the next best thing.

Sam crawled further between Matt's legs, his hip resting at Matt's crotch. "Are you ready to go up to bed with us?"

"Us?' Matt asked.

"Yeah, us," Isaac said.

Matt looked behind him and saw the shadow of Isaac leaning against the doorway. God, even in the dark Isaac was sexy as hell. He wanted to forget about the damn album and take the two men upstairs, but he knew it was time he told them something. They'd been patient enough with him, they deserved something in return.

"Can you come over? I need to talk to you both."

"Only if we can do some readjusting. I'm not about to sit on the other side of the patio and the way the two of you are sitting, there's barely a corner left for me," Isaac said, pulling Sam and Matt to their feet.

Being the biggest, Isaac sat in the lounge chair and gestured for Matt to sit between his spread thighs. Matt did the same thing for Sam. Matt found he liked this position much better. He could feel close to his lovers but not have to look them in the eye.

Leaning back against Isaac's chest, he passed the album to Sam. "I stole this."

"Huh?" Sam asked, taking the book. He waited for Sam to open it. No-one could see much in the moonlight, but enough to know what it was.

"It's not yours?" Isaac asked. "I'll admit to taking a peek at it earlier. It had me a little worried."

Matt wasn't angry with Isaac. He had a feeling when he sent Isaac after it that he'd look. A part of him wanted to know if Isaac would come back with disgust on his face, but then again, they didn't know the story.

"It belonged to my best friend, Danny."

"So, you weren't planning a wedding? Or...were you planning one with him?" Isaac asked.

"Oh, hell no. Danny was straight as an arrow. I was planning it with him though. It's something he did to keep the memories at bay, I think. We served on a medivac unit together. When you see death on a daily basis you need something to remind you of life."

Matt pointed towards the book. "That was Danny's way."

"So Danny was the one getting married," Sam said.

"He hoped. He hadn't proposed to his girl yet. He wanted to wait until he knew for sure he was going home. Danny and Julie had been high school sweethearts. They wrote each other daily, emailed as often as they could."

Matt shook his head. "I've never seen someone so in love. Hell, after two years serving side by side, I learned to love her, and I've always been gay," he chuckled, trying to lighten the mood.

Matt sobered. "Anyway, when Danny was killed, I stole the album. In the beginning I told myself it was so Julie didn't ever have to know, you know, so she could move on. Recently, I've decided I wasn't being gallant at all. I stole that book for myself. I'm a selfish sonofabitch, plain and simple."

He felt Isaac's arms tighten around him. "It's the only thing I have to keep Danny's memories alive. The only thing not tainted by blood and death."

"And you don't think Danny would've wanted you to have it?" Sam asked.

"No. He would've wanted it to go to Julie. I'd like to think he'd want me to keep it since the two of us worked on it together, but no." Matt kissed the top of Sam's head. "But he's dead, and I'm not. Guess he doesn't have much say anymore."

Isaac's arms tightened. "How did he die?"

Matt's mind saw the charred remains of his best friend. He shook his head, swallowing the sob that threatened to erupt. "I don't want to talk about that now."

"Okay, baby." Isaac ran his hands over Matt's chest.

"Can we eat now?" he asked. He just wanted to forget, to eat a quick dinner and fall asleep in the arms of his lovers. He'd deal with the past and the album later, but for now, he wanted to live and feel.

* * * *

Isaac watched Sam putter around the kitchen. They'd told him sandwiches were fine, but Sam wouldn't hear of it. He said they all needed comfort food, even if it was almost ten o'clock at night.

It was fine by him, he loved fried chicken. Still, the feel of Matt's thigh under the table was starting to give him very wicked thoughts. He determined one thing. First and foremost, Matt had on way too many clothes.

Isaac stood and started unbuttoning his shirt. "I say we eat naked." He watched as Matt's jaw dropped and Sam almost lost hold of the chicken he was turning. Good, he had their attention.

He quickly slid his shirt off his shoulders and went to work on his slacks. When he was totally nude, he spread his arms and looked from Matt to Sam. "Well, am I the only one who plans on enjoying his dinner?"

Matt started laughing. It was the first real smile Isaac had seen from him in days. Sam shook his head and chuckled. "You two go ahead, but I don't plan on burning my bits just to give you perverts a thrill."

"Guess it's just the two of us," Isaac said and tried to pull Matt into his lap.

Matt braced his hands on Isaac's shoulders. "I am not sitting on your lap. Number one, I'm too damn big, and number two, I'm a man, dammit."

Isaac narrowed his eyes and pushed Matt to the table. "Fine, sit up there, but I'm planning a little pre-dinner appetizer and you're definitely on the menu."

As Matt got himself comfortable, Isaac looked over at Sam, who was staring with his hands on his hips. "What?" Isaac asked.

Sam pointed his meat fork at Isaac. "You told me there wasn't anything emasculating about sitting on your lap."

Isaac couldn't help but laugh. "Seriously?" He looked at Matt and narrowed his eyes. "You'd better tell Sam that you were kidding." He subtly pinched Matt's thigh. "You haven't lived until Sam's squirmed naked in your lap. Trust me," he said with a slight nod.

Matt looked at Sam. "Isaac's right. I really was teasing."

Sam's eyes narrowed as he studied the two of them. Isaac had no doubt that it wouldn't matter if Matt had called Sam a sissy. Sam would still enjoy his rides on Isaac's lap, which was fine by him.

Sam made a mock disgusted sound in his throat and turned back to the stove. Isaac mouthed the words "Thank you" to Matt and received a wink in return.

Isaac stood and pulled Matt to the edge of the table. He wrapped his lover's legs around his waist and started grinding. "Nice," he said, rubbing his erection against Matt's.

"Mmm," Matt answered.

Isaac held Matt by the back of the head and kissed him, pushing his tongue deep. He wanted this man to know how much he needed him. He swept the interior of Matt's mouth as his free hand pinched and rubbed one of the prominent nipples on that well-developed chest he loved so much. "God you're sexy," he panted as he broke the kiss.

"Need you," Matt whispered, his green eyes attesting to his desires.

Isaac looked over at Sam. He was still cooking dinner like nothing carnal was happening on the kitchen table. "How long before dinner?"

Sam chuckled and shook his head. "When has dinner ever stopped you?" Sam turned around and grinned at Isaac. "Ten minutes until you need to set the table. Uh...leave time to thoroughly scrub it."

Isaac turned back to Matt. "Hear that? We've got nine minutes."

He laid Matt back on the table, and ran his hands over his torso. "So sexy," he said, bending to lick Matt's nipples. He worked his way down Matt's hard body, bypassing the bobbing cock to lave the heavy set of balls.

Matt bent his legs to rest his heels on the edge of the table giving Isaac a view of that pretty pucker. "Mmmm," he said, and ran his tongue over the ridged skin.

The ringing phone made them all jump. He looked over at Sam. It was never good news when a call came in so late at night.

"Dr. Browning," Sam said, answering the phone.

Isaac remained frozen, mouth an inch away from Matt's hole, waiting. "We'll be there, George." Sam hung up and turned off the stove. "Bad accident just outside of town on Gilmore Road," Sam said, quickly putting the chicken on a stack of paper towels. "George wants us at the accident scene until help arrives from Sheridan."

The three of them put their clothes on in minutes. Isaac turned to Matt. "You don't need to do this." No way would he put Matt's mental health in jeopardy.

"You're not leaving me behind," Matt replied, jaws tense.

There was something about the way it was said. Isaac knew this was not the time to argue with his lover. "Okay. I think we should drive two cars."

"Good idea," Sam said picking up two sets of keys from the counter. "Is your trunk still fully stocked?"

"Yeah. Did George say how many vehicles were involved?" Isaac asked, unlocking his car.

"Just two cars. George wasn't on the scene yet so he couldn't tell me how many people or the extent of the injuries."

Isaac nodded as Matt got in the front seat with him. Sam pulled out of the driveway first. Isaac backed out of the drive and headed towards the accident scene.

"You sure you're okay with this?" Isaac asked, placing a hand on Matt's thigh.

"I've had plenty of experience in triage. I won't let you down."

"I know you won't. I'm just worried about you," Isaac confessed.

Matt placed his hand on top of Isaac's. "I know, me too. But I can do this. I'll deal with the fall-out later."

By the time they arrived on the scene, Zac and Collin had already arrived to help George. Isaac popped the trunk and quickly got out of the car. He dug a big box of medical supplies out of the back of the car and handed it to Matt. "I'm sure Zac has a lot of this, but just in case."

"Which one is Zac?" Matt asked.

Isaac pointed to a man standing beside one of the wrecked vehicles. "That's him. The good-looking guy with dark hair. He's the town's paramedic."

Matt nodded. "I'll see what he wants me to do."

Isaac pulled out his big black leather bag as George came running up to him. "What've we got?" Isaac asked.

"One dead, two seriously injured, one with minor and one without a scratch." George started walking to the car with the most damage. "Zac is taking care of the other car. I see Sam and your physical therapist are helping him out."

"Alcohol?" Isaac asked.

George shook his head. "Hard to say." George stopped Isaac before they got to the car. "Um, Mitch Lanham was the driver, it looks like he was killed on impact. Hearn and my cousin, Tyler were both in the car. Hearn appears to have a broken leg and multiple cuts on his face and arms from the windshield. Tyler looks unharmed."

Damn. Mitch was never one of his favourite people, but he still new the guy. It was the hardest part about living in a small town. "How's Hearn taking it?" Mitch and Hearn had been partners for several years, although Isaac could never understand the dynamic of that particular relationship. Hearn was one of the nicest guys he knew, absolutely nothing like Mitch.

George grabbed a disposable blanket out of the fire truck as they made their way to the car. "You'll see. He's the one I'm really concerned with." He motioned Isaac to the passenger side. "Distract him while I cover Mitch."

Isaac squatted down in the open doorway. "Hi, Hearn."

Hearn didn't even look at him. "Hearn? It's Dr. Singer. I'm going to look at these cuts, see if I can get some of the bleeding stopped." He quickly dug in his bag and pulled out some sterile gauze. Ripping open the packages, he glanced into the back seat. Tyler sat with his head down. "You okay?" Isaac asked Tyler.

"Yeah," Tyler mumbled.

Turning his attention back to Hearn, Isaac began blotting blood, trying to assess the extent of the facial lacerations. He heard a helicopter overhead. "Hearn? The guys are here to take you into Sheridan. They'll get your leg fixed up."

Hearn still refused to acknowledge Isaac's presence. Yeah, the guy was definitely in shock. When the rescue squad reached Hearn, Isaac stepped back and opened the back door of the sedan. "Tyler?"

Tyler looked up, eyes wet. Isaac held out his hand. "Why don't you come with me? We'll let these guys work."

Tyler nodded and got out of the car. "How are the people in the other car?" Tyler asked.

"I'm not sure, but there are plenty of people working on them." He ushered Tyler to his car. "Why don't you have a seat?"

Isaac got Tyler settled on the soft leather, crouching down to talk to him. "I'm sorry, but I think the Sheriff's deputy needs to ask you a few questions. You seem to be the only one capable of answering at the moment."

"It was Mitch's fault," Tyler blurted out. He covered his mouth with his hand.

Isaac put a hand to the small man's shoulder. "I'll go get Deputy Roy and you can talk to him. If you'd like, I can drive you to the hospital in Sheridan once we get the scene taken care of."

Tyler nodded.

After telling Roy that Tyler was ready to talk, Isaac started making his way over to Matt and Sam who were now off to the side of the road. The closer he got the more he began to worry.

Matt's eyes seemed glazed and Sam was holding him, talking softly into Matt's ear. He suddenly wondered if they'd need to drive him to the hospital as well.

Chapter Eight

Isaac found Matt in his office with the door open. He leaned against the threshold, watching his lover for a few moments. Wearing his workout clothes with his tiny white tank top on, Matt was the epitome of male perfection. Isaac could tell by the pumped look of his biceps, he'd worked out only a few moments prior. His cock took notice of the prominent nipples, begging for his touch.

He shouldn't feel this horny. He and Sam had made it a habit to love Matt morning and night since the accident. It seemed to be the only time his lover was able to forget the blood and death he'd once been surrounded by. Because of that, he and Sam thought it best that Matt didn't attend Mitch's funeral services. Matt seemed to agree because he didn't oppose the suggestion. They had both cancelled their appointments for the day knowing Matt would probably need their presence.

"Hey," he finally said and stepped into the room.

Matt looked up, doing his best to smile. There had been so much sadness in his lover's eyes lately.

"How was it?" Matt asked. He got out of his chair and walked into Isaac's embrace.

Isaac closed his eyes, thankful once again that he had the chance to love this incredible man. "Hard." He kissed Matt's nose.

"How's Hearn dealing with it?" Matt asked.

Running his hands down Matt's back, he sighed. "He's decided to go and see his family back east for a while. I think Tyler's taking it harder than anyone."

He shook his head. "I'm not sure if it's Mitch's death or Hearn's leaving, but he's definitely not the friendly man we're all used to seeing around town."

"Where's Sam?" Matt asked.

Isaac smiled. "He's at the store getting picnic supplies."

"Picnic supplies?"

"Yeah, we thought we'd get out of town for the afternoon and take you to one of our favourite spots." He moved his hands to Matt's ass and squeezed. "It's very secluded. How do you feel about making love in a field of wildflowers?"

Matt licked Isaac's jaw, grinding his cock against him. "I've never done it, but it's something I'd definitely like to try."

The feel of Matt's erection rubbing against his own was too much temptation. Isaac slipped his hands under the elastic waistband of the workout pants. He was happy to feel sweet skin. Damn, he did love it when Matt wore a jock strap.

"Mmmm, I might need a little pre-picnic appetizer," Isaac said, running his fingers between the cleft of Matt's ass.

"Hmmm," Matt responded. "Your appetizers usually turn into full blown meals."

"Yeah, but I never seem to get full," Isaac returned. "You got stuff in here?"

"Drawer, top right."

Isaac walked him over to the desk, pushing Matt's sweats down as they went. The firm toned ass in his hands drove him wild. He quickly turned Matt around and pushed his torso down on the antique wood. "Need you bad," he said, opening the drawer.

Setting the lube on the corner of the desk, he unbuttoned his shirt and let it fall to the floor. His pants were next, which slid to his feet. Squatting behind Matt, he hooked a finger through the elastic strap of the jock and moved it to the side, making room for his questing tongue.

The musky flavour of his lover had his cock throbbing. He realised as much as he wanted to thoroughly devour Matt, his cock had other ideas. It wanted in now. Isaac ran his tongue over the loosening hole once more and reached for the lube. "Sorry, baby, I can't wait."

"Just fuck me," Matt answered.

Isaac slicked up his fingers and began stretching and probing Matt's hole. He found that all important walnut sized gland and ran his finger over it. While Matt was moaning, he quickly slipped two more in, knowing the bite of pain that would accompany such a quick invasion.

The pain only seemed to fuel Matt's desires. "Now…just…goddamn…do it now," Matt panted, rubbing his jock covered cock against the desk.

Isaac stood and positioned the head of his cock at Matt's hole. He gently pushed the crown past the first ring of muscles before plunging in fully as Matt cried out. It was a damn good thing the clinic was empty or they would have had nurses running.

He leaned over Matt's strong back and kissed him. Matt's head turned at an awkward angle, taking the kiss deeper. "I love you," Isaac whispered.

Matt closed his eyes. "I love you, too." He gave Isaac another soft kiss. "Now, move," Matt begged with a grin firmly planted on his face.

Chuckling, Isaac stood and put one hand to Matt's lower back as he gripped a smooth hip with the other. He pulled out several inches before pounding back in.

"Yes!" Matt shouted. "Harder."

Isaac gave his lover exactly what he'd asked for, powering in and out as hard as he could. He watched the muscles in Matt's back ripple and twitch, a sure sign he was close.

It felt good, knowing he could make a man so much younger feel good. Hell, it made him feel half his age. "Gonna," Matt grunted a moment before the muscles surrounding Isaac's cock squeezed.

The grip was so tight he had to wait for Matt's body to relax before he could continue. He knew he was close, but he also knew he had a few more thrusts in him. "So good," he said.

"Watching my cock pound this pretty ass," he panted, getting off on his own words. With one more plunge, Isaac buried his cock to the root and shot his lover full of his seed.

He felt the orgasm in every muscle and nerve as he continued to empty his balls. By the time Matt's body had milked him dry, Isaac was exhausted. What was he just thinking about feeling younger? He collapsed on Matt's back, completely sated but tired as hell.

It was then that it hit him. There was a huge age difference between him and Sam and Matt. Would he always have the stamina to satisfy such a young virile man? What if either him or Sam got sick? Would Matt love them enough to care for two old men?

He slid off Matt's back to the floor, still trying to regain his forty-seven year old breath.

"Hey, what's wrong?" Matt asked, sitting on the floor beside him.

"Nothing," Isaac answered and gave Matt a kiss. "We'd better get cleaned up. I'm sure Sam's probably waiting for us."

He started to get up, but Matt stopped him. "Is it Sam? Is that what you're worried about? Will he be mad that we've been doing this?"

Isaac felt his chest tighten. He pulled Matt into his arms. "No, baby. Sam loves you as much as I do. If this relationship between the three of us is going to work, we have to be confident in our love for one another. Sam knows how much I love him. Of course, I'm sure he'll give me hell. He already thinks I'm an old horn dog, this will be further proof."

Old, being the operative word. Damn, he needed to get himself out of this sudden funk. This picnic was about sharing something he and Sam loved with Matt, not about his sudden self doubts.

"I don't want to cause problems between the two of you. It's what scares me the most," Matt said, kissing Isaac's jaw.

With his hand to the back of Matt's head, Isaac captured his lips in an all consuming kiss. The kiss grew in intensity until Matt started rubbing against Isaac. Breaking their lip lock, Isaac looked into those pretty green eyes. "Let's clean up."

Matt nodded. He stood and held his hand out for Isaac. "Come on old man," Matt joked.

His lover didn't know how close he was to the truth.

* * * *

Sam watched as Isaac's car pulled down the dirt path that doubled as a road. He'd almost given up on them, but figured Isaac had Matt well in hand. His lover was insatiable lately. Sam wasn't about to complain a bit.

Bringing Matt into the fold of their love seemed to refuel fires between him and Isaac. It wasn't that they'd lost desire for each other over the years. They'd just seemed to work themselves into a bit of a rut. That was now a thing of the past as he and Isaac explored each other's bodies as if for the first time.

"Hey," Matt called out as he and Isaac walked hand in hand towards the blanket. "What an incredibly beautiful spot. Who owns it?"

"The town trust actually owns the land, but its part of the acreage Shep leases." Sam looked out over the picturesque stream running through the field of wildflowers. He knew for a fact that it was also a favourite location for some of the cowboys on The Back Breaker, including Shep.

Matt took his shirt off in the warm early summer sunshine and plopped down beside Sam. "How are you?" Sam asked, pulling Matt into his arms.

"Okay. I've done a lot of thinking and I'd like to try talking to Dr. Zook," Matt said, unbuttoning Sam's shirt.

"Really? That's fantastic," he said. He sat up enough to shrug out of the white dress shirt. He should've gone home after the funeral to change, but figured they wouldn't be in clothes long anyway. Seemed he'd been right as Isaac immediately started to undress.

He looked up at his long-time lover. Isaac was still gorgeous. His eyes zeroed in on the flaccid cock which hung between Isaac's legs and grinned. "I guess you two have already taken care of round one. That puts you one ahead of me."

Matt stiffened in his arms. "How did you know?"

Sam rubbed Matt's chest, paying particular attention to those sensitive nipples. "You're laying here without a shirt and Isaac's not hard yet. An easy deduction on my part," he answered.

"Are you mad?" Matt asked.

"Not at all. Although it means you both owe me one." The words barely made it out of his mouth when Isaac dropped down to his knees and buried his face in Sam's cloth covered crotch.

"I can take care of that," Isaac mumbled.

"Be my guest," he said, lifting his hips so his lover could remove his slacks. He moaned as Isaac swallowed his cock. "Ahhh, this is the life," Sam said, spreading his arms out on the blanket.

Matt soon joined Isaac, and Sam's cock was deliciously laved by two tongues. He didn't know if he'd ever felt anything so wicked as Matt's tongue running over his anus as Isaac continued to minister to his cock.

When he felt Matt's tongue stab into him like a tiny cock, he almost lost it. "Close," he warned.

Isaac grunted and picked up the pace, bobbing his head up and down Sam's length like he couldn't get enough. Two fingers thrust in his ass alongside the tongue and Sam lost it, shooting his seed down Isaac's throat.

Once he'd emptied his balls, Isaac crawled up Sam's body and kissed him, sharing the flavour of his own cum. Sam tapped Matt on the head and gestured for him to join them. The resulting kiss had his head spinning.

When they finally broke for air, Sam looked from Matt to Isaac. "If that's the treatment I can expect to receive, the two of you should fuck in private more often."

* * * *

It had been a perfect day as far as Matt was concerned. They'd napped, eaten and loved until the sun slipped over the ridge. The cooler air of evening had them slipping back into their clothes.

"Thanks for sharing this place with me," Matt said.

"There are so many things we want to share with you." Isaac looked at Sam and then back to Matt. "We want you to move in with us, permanently."

Matt was a little surprised to say the least. He knew feelings were developing between them at lightning speed, but moving in seemed like a big step. What if his doctors got tired of dealing with his issues?

"I think I need to work some stuff out first," he said. "It's not fair to the two of you."

Sam dropped the blanket he was folding and pulled Matt into his arms. "Fair has nothing to do with it. We love you. Besides, I think we have our own issues to deal with. We'll get through them together."

Matt looked deep into Sam's light blue eyes. "What issues? The two of you've been together forever. If there are issues, they must be because of me." *Shit, had his worries come to fruition? Was he screwing up Sam and Isaac's relationship?*

"I can't speak for Isaac, but I'm concerned about the age difference," Sam said.

"Me, too," Isaac chimed in. "Never more so than earlier when we were in your office." Isaac walked over and joined them in a three-way embrace. "Twenty and twenty-five years is a big age gap. Sam and I will grow into old men while you're still virile. Have you thought of that?"

"Have I thought about one or both of you dying? Hell yes, almost every day, but I've also thought a lot about my own mortality. I could get called back to Iraq any day."

Matt pulled away from his lovers and paced around the field, stepping on flowers as he went. "I've seen enough of it to know death doesn't discriminate. It doesn't matter if you're young or old, when it's your time, it's your time. All I know is that I love you both and I want to spend as much time…as many years with you as God allows."

He'd cheated death once, and he knew how lucky he was to be standing in front of these two men. It dawned on him how much the two of them deserved to have a whole man as their third, not the shell that he'd allowed himself to become.

His resolve firmly in place, he walked back and gave first Isaac and then Sam a kiss. "I'm calling Dr. Zook as soon as we get back to the house."

Isaac pulled out his cell phone. "Why wait until then?"

Chapter Nine

"Are you sure you gave me the right directions?" Matt asked Isaac. He switched the cell phone to his other ear and grabbed the map Isaac had drawn for him.

"Where are you at?" Isaac asked.

"I'm on Silver Canyon road. I just passed A22."

"You've gone too far. The map said to turn in the drive before A20."

Matt rolled his eyes. "There wasn't a driveway before A20."

"Sorry, baby, but there was. Turn around and go back. There will be a dirt track on the west side of the road."

Matt slowed and looked into his rear view mirror before making a U turn. Going back he cradled the phone between his ear and shoulder. "You secretly hate me, don't you?" he joked. "You know, you could've come with me."

"Yeah, I coulda, and I wanted to, but Sam said it was something you needed to do on your own."

Matt stopped the car. "Okay, I see what looks like a cow path."

"That would be it," Isaac chuckled.

"I take it he doesn't get out much," Matt said turning into the overgrown driveway.

"They," Isaac corrected.

Matt took the pitted road as slow as possible, his old car protesting with every pothole. "Ben's partner's in a wheelchair, had a stroke going on eight years ago. Since then, Ben has pretty much retired."

"So why did he agree to see me?" Matt asked. He wanted to know what he was getting himself into before reaching his destination.

"You'll see," Isaac said.

"I don't understand," Matt said as he pulled up to a rambling ranch house, complete with blood hound on the front porch.

"You will. Remember that Sam and I love you, and we'll be here when you need us."

Matt felt himself blush at the vow of love. "Love you both. Thanks for working through this with me."

"It's all part of loving someone. You enjoy the good and work through the bad."

Matt watched as the front door opened and the old dog rose to his feet. He looked into the eyes of BJ, the guy he'd been talking to at the bar. "Sonofabitch," he calmly said. "Did you set me up that day?"

Isaac chuckled. "Nope. When I walked into the bar and saw the two of you sitting together, I backed away. That's all I'll take responsibility for."

He suddenly felt more nervous than he had before. "I'll call you when I'm done."

"Relax. I doubt there's anything you can say to Ben that would surprise him."

"Bye."

"Bye, baby," Isaac said before hanging up.

He tossed the phone in the seat and took a deep breath. BJ stood on the porch scratching the dog's head like he had all the time in the world. *Okay, let's do this thing.*

* * * *

By the time they heard Matt's car pull into the drive, he and Isaac had almost driven each other crazy. Matt had been gone for hours.

Isaac started to get up, but Sam pulled him back down in his chair. "Give him a minute."

"A minute? He called over three hours ago to say he was leaving Ben's," Isaac growled.

Matt appeared around the corner of the house, his hands stuffed in his pockets. "Sorry," he said.

Sam stood and opened his arms. Matt walked straight to him and laid his head on Sam's shoulder. "I guess I should've called."

He looked at Isaac and gestured for his lover to join them. Soon, Matt was sandwiched between the two of them. Sam noticed Matt's hands were still in his pockets. Although he seemed to welcome the embrace, Matt was still partially closed down.

Sam decided the best thing was to give Matt the time he seemed to desperately need. He ran his hands in circles over Matt's back, feeling the beat of Isaac's pounding heart as he did so.

"I drove to that spot. You know, the one by the pond?"

"Yeah," Sam said, kissing Matt's soft lips.

"I just needed to work some stuff out, I guess."

"Nothing wrong with that," Isaac added, kissing Matt's neck.

Their kisses and touches weren't meant to arouse, but rather to comfort. Matt seemed so lost. Sam tried to take his queue from Matt. Whatever his lover needed, Sam had no doubt he and Isaac could provide.

After several minutes, Matt's hands slipped from their clenched position in his pockets, to wrap around Sam. "I need to go to Kansas," Matt whispered.

Sam felt his chest clench. Was his lover leaving them? "What's in Kansas?" he asked, afraid of the answer.

"Danny's home town," he answered.

"You want us to go with you?" Isaac asked.

"Yes." Matt sighed. "But it's something I need to do on my own. I thought I'd fly out Friday night and be back by Sunday evening."

"Will that give you enough time? Because you can take off as many days as you need," Sam said. He hated the thought of Matt going through it on his own, but admired his lover for knowing it was best.

"No. Two days should be plenty. I need to give Julie the album and explain my actions. I want to stop by and speak to Danny's folks, and I want to see his grave."

Sam pulled Matt even closer. That was a long list of emotional tasks to complete in one day. He didn't know many men that could go through that kind of day without a shoulder to lean on. He decided on the spot, that he wanted to be that shoulder.

"Let's go inside. I imagine you're starved," he said, taking a step back.

"Yeah, haven't eaten since breakfast," Matt said. He let Sam and Isaac lead him to the kitchen.

"Sandwich? Isaac and I didn't cook anything for dinner, so I don't have any leftovers to offer you."

Matt stopped and looked at him. "The two of you didn't eat? Because of me?"

Sam shrugged. "We grabbed what we could find. We just didn't feel like sitting down to a table of two." He leaned in and gave Matt a tender kiss. "We've kinda gotten used to a table of three."

As Matt stepped further into his arms, Sam heard Isaac open the fridge. "Do you think when I get back I could move my stuff in?" Matt asked.

Some of his tension drifted away. Part of him had been worried that Matt's visit with Ben would result in a different conclusion. He knew Ben enough to know the old doc wouldn't advise against a relationship, but he was sure he'd probably told Matt to really think about life altering decisions when he was under this amount of stress.

The request to move, informed him Matt had given their relationship a lot of thought while out by the pond. "On one condition," Sam said. "We move your stuff over after you eat your sandwich. That way, you'll wake up in your own home in the morning."

Isaac was suddenly beside them, plate in hand. He leaned down and kissed Matt. "Eat up."

* * * *

"One more set," Matt said.

"Geeze, are you trying to kill me?" Kyle asked, a wide grin on his face.

"Nope. I'm trying to strengthen your muscles. Tangling with a man Gill's size on a daily basis, you're gonna need them," he chuckled.

Kyle got that faraway dreamy look. "Yeah," he admitted with a smile and started another set of sit-ups.

They hadn't talked about why he'd left the wedding before it was over. Kyle seemed to sense that something had happened, but obviously wasn't one to pry. Still, outside of his lovers and Nate, Kyle was the best friend he had in Cattle Valley.

"I'm leaving for Kansas City in a couple of hours," he finally admitted.

Kyle paused only briefly. "What's in Kansas City?"

"My best friend's grave. Danny served with me and I thought it was time I paid my last respects. He grew up in a small town south of the city." Matt realised at that moment that was his main objective for the trip. He had a lot of explaining to do, but most of it was to Danny.

Kyle surprised him by placing a hand on his shoulder. "Tough. I'm sorry."

Matt nodded, acknowledging the sentiment. He felt tears begin to burn at the back of his eyes and quickly blinked them away. "I should've done it when I first returned from overseas."

"No," Kyle said and pulled himself up using his wheelchair. "You needed to do it when you were ready. If the guy was indeed your best friend, he'd understand."

Matt thought about that for a few moments. Would he? Did he? Sadly, he'd never know. Danny was easy going, but loyalty meant everything to him. Had he been loyal to his best friend's memory by stealing the album? No, he didn't think so, which is why he so desperately needed to set things right.

"Let's get you on the treadmill," he said, helping Kyle stand.

Once he had Kyle on the machine, Matt fiddled with the keypad. "Five minutes. I'm setting the speed higher, so I'll let you get by with a shorter duration."

Kyle rolled his eyes. "You're a real prince."

"I try," Matt chuckled.

After a few minutes, Kyle looked up at him. "So, how're things going with the Doctors?" Kyle panted.

"Good," he said. "I moved in a couple of days ago."

"No shit? That's great." Kyle walked for a few more moments. Matt could see the vein in Kyle's neck standing out in stark relief. No matter what he put this man through, Kyle never complained. Much.

He thought about the days and nights since he'd officially moved in. Evenings were his favourite. He loved cooking dinner with whoever made it home first. He grinned. As much as he enjoyed the three of them making love, he also appreciated the moments of one on one time.

After finishing up with Kyle, Matt went in search of one of his men. He'd need to leave for the airport in an hour and wanted to give Isaac and Sam proper goodbyes.

He knocked softly on Sam's door. "You busy?" He asked.

Sam shook his head and took off the tiny reading glasses he wore when working on charts. In two seconds, Matt was kneeling between Sam's spread thighs kissing him. "I wanted to say goodbye," Matt said, running his tongue across Sam's lower lip.

"I can't believe how much I'm going to miss you," Sam said, running his fingers through Matt's hair.

He could see the truth in Sam's eyes. That one look did more for cementing his relationship with Sam than any words could. "I love you," he whispered.

"I love you, too."

Matt slowly started unbuttoning Sam's shirt. "What time is your next appointment?"

Sam scooted a little lower in his chair. "Not for awhile. What did you have in mind?"

He kissed his way down Sam's chest, stopping to bite and lick those sweet protruding nipples. He released Sam's semi-hard cock and swiped his tongue across the crown. "I want to leave Cattle Valley with the taste of your cum in my mouth," Matt said with a grin.

The thought of being able to taste his lover while riding on a plane, fuelled his desires even more. Without waiting for an answer, Matt slid his lips over the fat cock in his hand. Sam made that soft moaning sound Matt loved and insinuated his leg between

Matt's, pressing against his swollen cock, still trapped in his pants.

He swirled his tongue around the ridged crown before dipping into the wide slit at the top. Matt was rewarded with a large dollop of sweet tasting pre-cum. His hands pushed Sam's slacks to his ankles as he sank further down the shaft.

With his lover further exposed, Matt's hands began to knead Sam's heavy sack. "Matty," Sam called out when Matt pressed a finger to the sensitive spot behind Sam's balls.

Matt grinned around the cock in his mouth. Sam only called him by that particular nickname when he was about to cum. He picked up his pace, swallowing as much of Sam's length as he could before quickly withdrawing and going down again. His middle finger rubbed against Sam's puckered hole.

"Shit," Sam grunted.

He loved the way his lover's thighs quivered under his forearms. He opened his throat further, knowing Sam would shoot at any second, and thrust a finger inside, going straight for the smooth pleasure gland.

The first jet of seed filled his mouth. Matt backed off enough to swallow the creamy essence as he continued to move his finger in and out of Sam's hole. Sam pressed his leg harder against Matt's cock. Matt barely managed to fumble his own pants open before he shot his own load.

When he'd milked Sam's cock dry, Matt let it slip from his mouth. He licked the few tendrils of cum that had escaped his mouth earlier. "I can't believe I went over two years without sex. Now the prospect of going two days without it is almost enough to change my mind about leaving."

"We could still come with you," Sam said, pulling Matt up into his arms to share a kiss.

Matt shook his head. "You'd never forgive yourselves if something happened in town and they were left without a doctor on hand. I'll call you before I get to sleep each night and you can talk dirty to me. Better yet, put the phone on speaker and make love to Isaac. There's nothing that turns me on more than the sound of him slamming into you."

Sam smiled. "He does tend to get a little loud." His lover's face suddenly fell. "Our bed will feel empty without you."

Matt wrapped the words around him. He knew he'd need every ounce of strength in the coming days, and Sam's and Isaac's love did a lot to fuel his heart. His eyes caught the time on Sam's watch. He hated to leave his lover, but… "I need to go say goodbye to Isaac."

Sam kissed him again, their mouths fused, their tongues thrusting and tasting. When they pulled back for a much needed breath, Sam chuckled. "You know Isaac isn't going to be satisfied with a blow job."

"Yeah," Matt grinned. Isaac loved bending him over his big desk. It was something he'd learned to count on in the afternoons.

Chapter Ten

"Hey, dude, how're you feeling?" Danny asked.

"Sick as a dog," Matt answered from his bunk. He couldn't remember ever feeling as bad in his life. Three days in this stupid tent in this stupid bunk and he was about to go crazy.

His unit had been kept so busy with the increased bombings on the outskirts of the city, Matt hadn't even had anyone to talk to. He saw the effects of the previous several days on his buddy's face. Death took a heavy toll and it looked like Danny was at the end of his rope.

He suddenly felt guilty. There were men out there dying and here he was, lying safe in his bed because of a stupid virus. He tried to sit up. "I need to start pulling my weight again."

Danny pushed him back down. "You're sick and weak as a kitten. How long do you think you could administer CPR? I know you mean well, Matt, but let Jones continue to cover for you until you get your strength back."

His friend held up a finger and walked off. He was back in seconds holding several magazines. "Got these in the mail.

Your mission for the day is to find a honeymoon spot perfect for me and my girl."

Matt rolled his eyes, scanning the travel magazines in his hands. "Tropical and secluded?"

Danny shook his head. "Not unless it's on US soil. Once I get back to the States, I don't plan on ever leaving."

They heard Danny's name being called and the whirl of the Blackhawk coming to life. "Gotta go," Danny said. "I expect a full itinerary when I return."

"Sure thing," Matt reached out and grabbed his best friend's hand. "Watch your back."

"That's your job," Danny joked. "That's why you'd better hurry and get better." Danny turned and jogged out of his tent.

Matt didn't know how long he searched through the magazines before a Colonel stepped into his tent. Matt looked up from an article on Philadelphia. The look on his commanding officers face said it all. "What happened?"

Matt awoke to the captain coming over the loud speaker. He wiped the sweat from his face and looked around. No one seemed to be paying him attention so he must not have called out in his sleep at least.

He looked out the plane's small window at the patchwork landscape below. So this was the land Danny had loved. Matt felt a lump form in his throat. He wondered if he could see his friend's hometown from here.

"Are you from here?" the elderly lady beside him asked.

"No, ma'am." Matt shook his head. "I'm visiting a friend."

* * * *

The small town of Gardner, Kansas was easy to find, straight off I35. Matt pulled into the only hotel in town and turned off the ignition to the small rental car. He looked around at the full parking lot and shook his head. Why a place this size would have so many out of town visitors was beyond him. He was glad Isaac had taken the time to make him a reservation though.

Unfolding his legs from the cramped quarters of the car, Matt stretched. An hour drive didn't sound like much, but between the small space and the uneasy feelings, he felt wiped out.

He made his way inside, stepping up to the front desk. "Yes, I have a reservation under the name Matthew Jeffries."

He expected the clerk to search his computer, but was surprised when the guy smiled. "It's so nice to meet you, Mr. Jeffries. We've been expecting you."

Matt was stunned. "Huh?"

"Julie told us to take good care of you while you're in town."

Damn, this was a small town. He'd called Danny's parents after making his plane reservations. It had been an awkward conversation to say the least. He'd had to refuse Connie's and George's offer of a ride from the airport explaining he had several places he wanted to see and a rental car would be his best option. They seemed to take it in stride, but Matt couldn't help but to feel he'd hurt them in some way. Evidently, the McDougal's must still keep in contact with Julie. That was good. It would make Danny happy knowing his family still cared about his girl.

"Mr. Jeffries?"

Matt shook his head. "Sorry. Just a little surprised that Julie told you I was coming and that you gave a shit."

The clerk, Matt looked at the guys name tag, Steve it said his name was, looked confused. "Danny was very well liked. The entire town mourned his death. Of course we'd care that his best friend was coming to pay his respects."

He felt like a complete ass. "I apologise, Steve. This is all a little hard for me. I didn't mean to be rude."

Steve looked at him for several moments before waving a hand in the air. "Don't worry about it. I'll just get your key and the paperwork for you to sign."

Steve turned around and went to the desk off to the side. Several moments later he was back, key and paperwork in hand. "If you'll just sign here you'll be all set." Steve also laid an envelope on the counter in front of Matt. "Julie asked me to give this to you when you got in."

After signing, Matt picked up the envelope. His name was written in a fancy script on the front in purple marker. There was that lump in his throat again. He stuffed the envelope into his carryon bag. Matt picked the key card up from the counter and nodded his head. "Thanks for everything."

"No problem. Welcome to Gardner."

Matt slung his carryon over his shoulder and headed down the hall to the elevator. The hotel only had three floors. He pushed the button knowing he should just walk up to the second floor, but what the hell.

Before setting his bag down, Matt pulled the envelope out. Walking over to sit on the king-sized bed, he fingered the flap. Was he ready for this? The answer eluded him for several long moments.

With a sigh, he finally ripped it open and took out a single piece of lavender stationary.

Hi Matt, I'm hoping you aren't too tired after your flight. I'd love for you to meet me at The Oasis. Ask Steve for directions. I'll be there around eight.
Julie.

He tossed the note to the nightstand and lay back on the bed. He knew he wasn't ready to talk to her yet. His eyes sought out his bag, the red album tucked safely inside. No, no way was he ready to part with that yet.

He pulled out his cell phone and called home.

"Hello?" Isaac answered.

"Hey, it's me."

"Hey, baby. How was the flight?"

Matt felt like crying. He didn't know if it was hearing his lover's voice or being overly tired to deal with the residents of Gardner. "Flight was okay."

"What's wrong?" Isaac asked.

"People act like they know me here. Julie's already sent me an invitation to meet her some place in town for a drink."

"That's good."

Matt's jaw dropped. "What? How can you say that? I don't know these people."

"Calm down. It's good because it means that Danny talked about you to them. It's good because even though you don't see it, you're surrounded by people who care. Even if they only care because Danny did, it's something."

"I'm not ready to give Julie the album," he confessed.

"So don't," Isaac said matter-of-factly. "Take the chance of getting to know her before you decide what to do with the book."

"You think I should meet her?"

"I do. Does that make me a traitor?" Isaac asked.

Did it? "No, I guess not."

"So you'll go?"

Matt looked at the small digital clock beside the bed. "Probably. I need to take a shower and change out of these wrinkled clothes."

"Call when you get home, no matter what time it is."

Matt smiled. "I doubt I'll be staying out late. Besides, you're two hours behind me."

Isaac groaned. "And you know how much I love being behind you."

Matt chuckled for the first time since he'd arrived in Kansas. "I miss you," he said.

"Miss you, too. Go out and show Julie and the rest of the town what Danny saw in you."

"Thanks, Isaac."

"We'll be waiting for your call," Isaac said and hung up.

Matt shut his phone and tossed it on the bed. "The Oasis," he whispered. He wondered what kind of place it would be. He assumed jeans would be dressy enough. The town didn't strike him as being overly formal.

Getting off the bed, Matt opened his bag and removed the album, setting it aside. He pulled out a clean pair of jeans and underwear and a black sports shirt. He hoped he wasn't making a mistake. What would the friendly people of the town think if they knew he'd not been there to watch their favourite son's back?

* * * *

He pulled the rental car in front of the small downtown bar and wiped the ever-present sweat from his forehead. It wasn't hot, Matt knew it was his nerves playing havoc with him, but even after a cold shower he continued to perspire.

After locking the car, he gripped the handle and swung the door open. He almost ran back out when a group of people cheered his name. His heart started beating a mile-a-minute as he looked at the friendly faces gathered at the long table along the east wall of the bar.

A pretty brunette he recognised from countless pictures moved towards him. "I'm so glad you came," Julie said, giving him a big hug.

Matt knew if he thought too much about the friendly gesture he'd break down in tears. Instead he gave Julie a quick hug and stepped back. "You look just like your pictures," he said, trying to cover his awkward feelings.

Julie ran a hand over her shoulder length hair, smoothing it back into place. "I wish I could say the same to you, but the only picture I have is one from Danny's personal effects."

Matt knew immediately what picture she was referring to. He and Danny had just come from a long night of transporting soldiers to the hospital. One of the guys in their unit was snapping pictures to send home to his family and captured Matt and Danny's fatigue as they walked through the door. The guy had later given them both a copy of the picture. It was the only one he had of his best friend.

"I have the same picture," he told Julie.

"Well, I'm happy to say that you look much better in person," she grinned and kissed his cheek.

She turned back towards the table of people. "These are some of Danny's closest friends. They wanted to meet you, too. I hope you don't mind?"

Hell yeah he minded, but what could he say. He nodded and let Julie walk him to the table. "Everyone, this is Matthew Jeffries." Julie then proceeded to go around the table and introduce the individuals.

Matt knew he'd never remember their names even though a few of them were very familiar. Yeah, these had been the buddies Danny had so often spoken of. Matt wondered if his own homecoming would've been different if he'd had a close network of friends like this. Would they have been able to help rid him of the constant guilt?

A tall beer was placed in front of him, and Matt eagerly started drinking it. Julie sat on the chair beside him. His unease must have been apparent because she reached over and threaded her fingers through his.

He was thankful the group didn't ask him about his time in Iraq. Evidently they knew not to ask questions unless information was freely given. Instead, the friends told stories about Danny. It was apparent they'd all known him all their lives. Matt listened and even managed to share a few of his own.

Julie, the rock, held his hand the entire evening. Several times he'd felt her squeeze his hand and when he'd looked at her tears were evident, but never did they fall. By closing time, Matt felt even closer to his old friend by listening to the way his life impacted others. No wonder the entire town mourned his death.

Everyone insisted on giving him a hug before he took off. Julie was the last to step into his arms. "Thank you. You'll never know what this meant to me," she whispered in his ear.

By the time he arrived back at his hotel, Matt had shed more than one tear. He undressed quickly and got in bed, reaching for his phone.

Damn he wished he hadn't been so strong headed. He really needed to be in the arms of the men he loved. He dialled home, knowing it was the closest thing possible.

Chapter Eleven

Matt had never been so happy to see the sun come up. He'd been sitting in front of the window since around three, unable to get back to sleep after yet another nightmare. He'd hoped coming to Kansas would ease them, but it didn't seem that way.

Glancing at the clock, he saw it was almost six-thirty. God he wanted to call Sam and Isaac, but he'd kept them up late the previous night and knew it wouldn't be fair. They'd done their best to soothe his sorrowful ass, but as soon as he'd hung up, he knew it hadn't been enough.

He got to his feet and headed towards the shower. He was supposed to have a late breakfast with Connie and George, but decided he'd drive around town for a while first. Hell, it wasn't like he would be sleeping in. He wondered if Danny's parents had purposely made the meeting late in the morning because they knew of Julie's plans the previous night.

Even taking his time in the bathroom, it was only seven when he picked his keys up from the dresser and hung the 'Do not disturb' sign on the door. He used the back flight of stairs to get down to the parking lot. He didn't know if Steve was working, but he wasn't in the mood to be civil.

In less than an hour, he'd driven down every street in town at least once. He even went as far as to drive by the new high school outside of town that Danny had mentioned. He still had an hour and a half to kill before meeting the McDougal's.

His eyes flicked towards the direction of the town cemetery. Maybe he should get it over with? Even as he thought it, he shook his head. No, he definitely wasn't ready to say goodbye, not yet at least.

It was still a little early to call his men, but decided they might forgive him this once. It was only forty-five minutes early. He hit speed dial and waited, his eyes continually looking in the direction of the cemetery.

"Hello?" a sleepy Sam answered.

"I'm sorry I woke you," he said.

He heard sheets rustling in the background. "Don't be ridiculous. We told you to call day or night if you needed to talk."

"I know, but I didn't really think you'd appreciate a call at one in the morning."

"Bad dream?" Sam asked.

"Several." Matt rubbed his eyes. God he was tired. "I've been up since three."

"Why didn't you go back to sleep?"

Matt yawned. "I didn't have the two of you to keep the demons away." He chuckled when he said it, but he knew it was closer to the truth than he cared to admit out loud.

"We miss you," Sam said.

"I shouldn't have told you that you couldn't come. I guess I thought I was stronger than I really am."

"Bullshit," Sam said. "You're facing your demons head on. It takes a lot of guts to do that, with or without support from people who love you."

"Tell me?" It was a very high school thing to ask, but he desperately needed to hear the words.

"I love you," Sam whispered, his voice dropping.

Matt could tell his man was getting emotional. He suddenly felt bad. The last thing he wanted was to bring Sam's mood down. "Thank you. You have no idea what that means to me."

"I think I do," Sam answered.

The two of them continued to talk for the next thirty minutes. "I'd better let you go so you can get your run in before you leave for the clinic."

"You're more important than any run, besides, it's an easy day. I'm only working until noon."

"Well, I need to start making my way to The Downtowner to meet the McDougal's."

"I'll have my cell on me all day. Call if you need to talk."

"I will. I love you." There was that damn lump in his throat again. He swore he was going to have to get that checked out when he got home.

"Love you," Sam said and hung up.

Looking at the clock, he determined he still had twenty minutes to get his act together before meeting Danny's parents. His mind went to the album. He was supposed to have dinner with Julie, but first he wanted to talk to Danny.

* * * *

Sam snuggled back against Isaac. He knew his lover wasn't asleep even though he'd said nothing during his entire phone conversation with Matt. "I think you need to go to him."

Isaac kissed Sam's neck. "Is he having a hard time?"

"Yes. I think he needs one of us and you know we can't both go without making preparations to get a substitute doctor in." He felt Isaac's morning erection press against his ass. His Isaac always woke horny. He was ashamed to say it, but before Matt came into their lives, he used to make sure he was up and running before Isaac woke.

It wasn't that he hadn't enjoyed sex, but Isaac would've happily had it two times a day if he could. He always felt he wasn't enough in that department for his lover, but Isaac had never strayed.

Since Matt came into the fold, their love making had improved dramatically. He thought it was partially due to the fact he loved to watch Isaac fuck their young lover. Maybe he was more of a voyeur than he'd ever realised.

He felt Isaac turn away for a moment before cool lubed fingers delved into the crease of his ass. They'd made love the previous night over the speaker phone, so he knew it wouldn't take much stretching to ready him.

"Why do you want me to go instead of you?" Isaac asked, sliding the head of his cock through the first ring of muscles.

"I think Matt needs you," he answered as Isaac slowly pushed in to the root. His lover started a gentle rhythm in and out of his body as they talked. This was the kind of sex he preferred and Isaac knew it, otherwise he'd be pounding in and out at lightning speed.

"You're the one he always seems to talk to when he's down," Isaac said. Sam could hear a trace of resentment in Isaac's voice.

"You're the one he goes to when he wants to forget about everything," Sam acknowledged. "You have the ability to consume a person's thoughts. I think that's what he needs."

Isaac's pace picked up, still not fast, but fast enough for his lover to get off. Sam reached down and wrapped his fingers around his shaft, riding the waves of pleasure Isaac was providing.

As always, Isaac started to let his passion get the better of him and hooked his arm under Sam's knee, opening him even further. "Come for me," Isaac moaned.

As if on command, Sam's cock shot silky strands of cum onto his fist and white sheets. Isaac hiked Sam's leg higher and thrust hard and deep until his body stiffened and he cried out Sam's name.

His leg was released and Isaac wrapped himself around him. "Love you," Isaac panted. They lay in comfortable silence for several moments before Isaac spoke. "Do you ever regret it?"

Regret it? Sam turned in Isaac's arms to face him. "What, me and you, or Matt and us?"

"Both, either."

Sam shook his head and kissed his lover of over twenty years. "Not even for a day."

"Not even a day? In all these years?" Isaac asked, his black brows shooting up.

Sam really thought about it. "I can't lie and say there weren't periods when I didn't feel as close to you. But you know, love is a cycle. You're my best friend in the world and have been for as long as I care to remember."

"But?"

"I've been worried for a couple of years that you'd find someone else," Sam admitted.

"What? Have I ever given you the impression that I'd cheat?" Isaac's voice was starting to get loud, not a good sign.

"No. I knew you'd never cheat. It's just that, well, I'm fifty-two. I don't want sex every day. Hell, I don't know if I ever did, even in my twenties."

Isaac's roaming hand stilled. "Is that why you agreed to invite Matt into our relationship?"

Was it? He'd done a lot of soul searching lately about that very question. "Yes and no, I think. It doesn't mean I don't love him, because I do, with all my heart. The two of us just need to express our love differently. Doesn't mean either of us are right or wrong. But for you, the act of making love is a necessity, an internal drive."

Isaac pulled away. "You make me sound like a goddamn sex addict." There was disgust in his voice.

"No," Sam said reaching out to his lover. *Fuck, he was really screwing this up*. The more he talked, the deeper in the hole he dug himself. "You're too much man, physically, for me. But I can't let you go, and I need you to be happy and satisfied. I show my love more through stupid stuff like cooking dinner, or doing your laundry."

"And Matt?"

"Matt's easy to love. He's gentle and kind." He glanced up at Isaac. "And I'll admit, sexy as hell. I may be old, but I'm not dead."

Isaac started to say something, but Sam stopped him. "I love making love with the two of you, never doubt that for a second. My love for him is completely genuine and given freely."

He could tell Isaac was still upset, but he figured he'd better stop while he was ahead. Trying to explain twenty years worth of worries and hidden feelings was never easy, and he was doing a horrible job of it. Maybe later, when things had calmed down he could try again.

He watched as Isaac pulled away and swung his legs over the side of the bed. "If I'm going to hop on a plane to Kansas, I'd better get my shit together," Isaac said without turning around.

Sam looked at Isaac's muscled back. He hoped to hell he hadn't just screwed up the best thing that had ever happened to him.

* * * *

Sitting in his car, across the street from the diner, Matt watched the townspeople go in and out the front door. He was already five minutes late for his meeting with Connie and George.

What would he say to them? "I'm sorry I was too sick to watch your son's back?" He wondered if they even knew he hadn't been with Danny when he was shot by a sniper's bullet.

He opened the car door. Whether they knew or not, he owed them his condolences. He knew that had the shoe been on the other foot, Danny would've gone straight to his parents' house upon his return to the States. Not waited almost six months.

He stepped into the diner and looked around as everyone seemed to turn to check out the newcomer. The waitress smiled and waved for him to follow her. Of course she'd known he was the outsider who was having breakfast with the McDougal's.

When he reached the table, both Connie and George stood. He was immediately embraced by two thin arms.

"It's so nice to finally meet you. Danny talked about you in every letter home." Connie pulled back and looked up into Matt's face. "It almost feels like I already know you."

Matt saw the tears shimmer in her brown eyes as she stepped back enough for George to approach. George's hand stretched out towards him. "Good to have you here," he said.

Matt shook the older man's hand. "Nice to meet you both."

George gestured to the table. "Would you like a cup of coffee?"

"Yes, please," he said, and turned the cup on the table upright.

Connie started to say something but stopped and covered her mouth. She picked up her over-sized purse and dug out a tissue as she started to cry.

Matt's gut twisted. He prayed he'd make it through their meal without falling to his knees and begging the McDougal's for their forgiveness.

Chapter Twelve

Matt refused George's offer to accompany him to the cemetery. Even though he'd no doubt have to scour the area for Danny's grave, it was something he needed to do alone. Connie had shared with him several of Danny's letters home and they still weighed heavily on his mind.

No wonder these people treated him like a hero. Danny had made him sound so much better than he really was. His friend even went as far as to tell his parents Matt was like a brother to him.

Matt got out of the car and tucked the well-travelled album under his arm. Did brothers have dreams of kissing each other? Of holding each other when the night skies were lit up with fire?

He started slowly down the first row of the northeast section. George had told him that's where he'd find Danny's final resting place. He didn't have to walk far before spotting it. Up ahead was a headstone surrounded with flowers and other trinkets he couldn't distinguish from his location. It had to be Danny's though. The numerous American flags planted on the newly grown grass.

Stepping up, Matt looked down "Daniel Eugene McDougal" *Eugene?* He couldn't help but to smile. Had he known that was Danny's middle name he would've done a whole lot more teasing.

Knowing he'd be there a while, Matt sat cross legged on the ground. He chuckled at the Miller Lite beer bottles, no doubt left by his numerous friends. He remembered Danny being shocked that Matt had never heard of the tradition. Now, as he looked at the surrounding headstones, he could see for himself what Danny had talked about. There were trinkets left on several graves, everything from beer to little statues. He even spotted a box of donuts on one. Danny's had more than any of them. "You're a very popular guy, Daniel Eugene McDougal," he said.

He picked up a snapshot pressed between two pieces of plastic laminate. He recognised the location. It was a picture of Danny in The Oasis surrounded by his friends. They were all holding up beers in an apparent toast. The sign in the background signifying Danny's going away party.

Matt wiped the moisture from his eyes. "I met most of your buddies at the bar. Nice people." His nose started to drip and he wiped it with the bottom of his shirt. "It takes a hell of a guy to have friends like that."

I bet they wouldn't have let you down the way I did. He cleared his throat and leaned the picture against the black granite base.

He glanced at the book in his lap and knew he'd put it off as long as he could. "I guess you can see that I brought your book back. Is that why you've been haunting my dreams? Because I stole it."

He opened the album to the last section. "I finished that honeymoon itinerary you wanted. I got to thinking about it, and decided you and Julie should see all the things we were over there fighting for."

Matt held the pages up to the gravestone. "I thought maybe you should start out in Philadelphia and work your way to Washington DC. I tried to fit a side trip to Mount Rushmore in there, but well, South Dakota isn't a side trip to anywhere."

He closed the book and laid it in the grass. "I thought I'd give it to Julie when I have dinner with her later. I know it would've gone to her anyway. I...I just needed a piece of you for a while."

Matt shook his head, the tears flowing freely down his cheeks. "Who am I kidding? I wanted a piece of you forever. I loved you, Danny. I'm ashamed of myself for it. You were one of the few guys who knew about me. But you never treated me differently, not once, and I took advantage of that friendship and fell in love."

He put his hands on top of the headstone and placed a kiss to the cold granite. There was so much more he wanted to say, but he knew he couldn't go on without completely breaking down. He still had the dinner to get through. Maybe he'd have time in the morning to stop by before he left for the airport.

"Julie will be expecting me before long. I spent too much time with your folks. Kinda got me off schedule. She's looking good, by the way. I can tell she misses you and I reckon you talk to her a hell of a lot more than you do me, but well, I thought I'd tell you that."

Matt picked up the red album. "I'll get this to its rightful owner. I love you, and I'll talk to you later," he said.

He stood and took one more look at his friend's name and smiled. "Eugene," he chuckled and shook his head.

* * * *

By the time he got back to the car and pulled himself together, it was almost four. He knew if he was going to get back to the hotel and get cleaned up he needed to leave, but he just couldn't seem to start the car.

A knock on his window made him jump. He looked over and came face to face with one of the guys he'd met at the bar. Roger? Rod? Rodney! That was the guy's name. Matt rolled down his window. He hoped he looked better than he felt. "Hey," he said.

Rodney held up a package of beef jerky. "I just came from the lake. There's a little convenience store down there that sells this." Rodney shrugged. "It was Danny's favourite, so I thought I'd sit with him a spell and share it."

Matt felt that thick lump form in his throat once more. "I'm sure he'll appreciate that," he said.

Rodney looked at Matt for several long minutes. "You feeling guilty?"

The air whooshed out of his lungs like he'd been sucker punched. "Does it show?"

Rodney nodded. "Mostly in the eyes. The way you can't seem to look at any of us when you talk."

Matt couldn't help it. He buried his face in his hands. "We always watched each other's backs and we always came back safe. I wasn't there the day he was killed. I was in bed sick."

He expected to hear disgust in Rodney's voice. He knew he deserved it so he braced himself. When Rodney didn't say a word, Matt looked up, expecting Rodney to have walked off.

Instead, Danny's friend opened the package of jerky and handed him a piece. "Sounds like he was damn lucky to have you on all those other missions." Rodney shrugged and bit into the dried beef. "The only one who blames you for Danny's death is you. Danny wouldn't have. We both know that."

"He was a much better person than I am," Matt said, trying to chew the peppered beef.

"Yep," Rodney said. "But then again…Danny was a better person than anyone I've yet to meet."

Lord wasn't that the truth. Setting the rest of his jerky on the seat beside him, Matt opened the car door and pulled Rodney into a hug. It seemed at that moment Rodney needed the contact as much as he did.

After several moments they broke apart. No more words were spoken between them. Matt got back into his car and started the engine. He gave Rodney a wave as he pulled out of the cemetery.

* * * *

Sitting in front of the small Mexican restaurant, Matt felt the emotion of the day weigh on his shoulders. He didn't know if he'd ever cried so much in his life.

He picked up the paper sack beside him. He'd decided it would be better not to just plop a book of memories on the table in front of Julie upon arrival. Instead, he'd asked the desk clerk for a bag to put the album in.

He was immediately shown to his table, where Julie sat smiling. He noticed her eyes looked puffy, a sure sign she'd been crying. *Join the club.* He bent and gave her a kiss on the cheek before taking his seat.

"How are you?" She asked. There was nothing but pure concern in her hazel eyes.

"Tired," he said honestly. He set the paper sack on the floor beside his chair. "Been a long couple of days."

Julie nodded. They placed their drink orders and Matt picked up his menu. "What's good?"

"The shredded beef burritos. That's what I always get," she answered. She picked up the salt shaker and looked at the big bowl of chips. "Do you mind?"

Matt smiled and shook his head. "Not at all." He set his menu aside as his jumbo-sized margarita was set in front of him.

Julie moaned as she swallowed a drink of her strawberry daiquiri. "Man I needed that," she said with a grin.

"It looks like it's been a rough day for you as well," he commented.

"Yeah, well, it's certainly been a cathartic couple of days." Julie reached across the table and squeezed Matt's hand. "I have something for you, but I'm not sure when to give it to you."

Matt thought of the package beside his feet. "I have something for you as well."

Julie looked into her glass. "I've got an idea. Let's drink up and get out of here."

He wasn't sure what she had in mind, but he agreed this wasn't the place for the things he needed to discuss with her. He nodded and they both drank their drinks. Julie put her fingers to her temples. "Ooh, brain freeze," she chuckled.

When they were both finished, he put enough money on the table to pay for their drinks and tip before picking up his package. He led Julie out of the restaurant. "Would you like for me to drive?" he asked.

"Will you think I'm crazy if I ask you to meet me at the cemetery?"

He didn't want to tell her that he wasn't ready to go back yet. It was obvious this was important to Julie, and he decided the night would be for her. Danny would've wanted it that way. "Sure."

"Great," she said with a smile. "I've got a few supplies to gather, but I'll be there as soon as I can."

"I'll wait for you," he said.

* * * *

"Hello?" Sam answered.

"Hey, how's it going?" Matt asked.

"Fine. I just finished stitching Jeremy Lovell's cheek."

"Damn, what happened?" Just the sound of Sam's voice put Matt at ease. Familiar and warm, he could almost feel Sam's arms wrapped around him.

"Fight I guess. He's not talking. He'd gone to Gillette to see his old man ride. Came back early with a black eye and a nasty cut on his cheek. Shep brought him in.

He figures the kid hit on the wrong cowboy and is too embarrassed to talk about it."

"That'd do it," Matt agreed.

"So, how're you feeling?" Sam asked.

He thought about it for several moments. "Matt?"

"Yeah, I'm here. I'm just not sure how I'm doing. I had a nice visit with Danny earlier, tough, but nice. I'm sitting in my car at the cemetery as we speak. Julie's meeting me here."

"You up for that?"

"Nope, but I think it's something she needs." Matt rubbed a hand over his face.

"You're a good man."

"No I'm not, but Danny was, and I owe him this."

"Stop it. What happened overseas was not your fault. The fact that you didn't die along with your friend doesn't make you any less a good man. I'm getting damn tired of hearing you talk like that."

Matt sat up. He didn't know if he'd ever heard Sam this angry. "Sorry," he said automatically. He saw Julie pull up behind his car. "Sam?"

"Don't apologise. I'm the one who should be doing that. I didn't mean to lose my temper. It's just killing me to see you continue to beat yourself up. War sucks. People die. Good people. But it's not your fault."

"Okay. Um, I need to go," Matt said. He was still feeling a little off kilter.

"Call me before you go to bed."

"I will. I love you."

"I love you, too. Hurry back to me," Sam said and hung up.

Matt took a deep cleansing breath before opening the car door. Julie was pulling sacks out of the car, a blanket tossed over her shoulder.

"Here, let me help you," Matt said, and took the bags from her arms.

"Thanks. I hope you like burgers?" she asked holding up a greasy looking sack.

"Love 'em."

Together they walked to Danny's grave. Julie spread out the blanket and sat on one corner. "Make yourself comfortable." She pulled burgers and onion rings out of the bag. "Hoch's has the best cheeseburgers."

Matt took his food and set it in front of him. He dug into one of the sacks he'd carried and got them both out a bottle of Miller Lite. Passing over the beer, he gestured to the ones beside the stone. "Did you bring all those here?"

Julie shook her head. He watched as tears pooled in her eyes and felt like a piece of shit. "I didn't mean to…"

"You didn't," she said, wiping her eyes. She pointed to the bottles. "Those actually aren't for Danny, they're for me. Danny's friends leave them here in case I need a drink when I come to sit with him."

Damn, there goes that lump. "Do you come here often?" He hated to think of Julie alone in the cemetery drinking her life away.

"Not as much as I used to, but once in a while." Julie set down her hamburger and wiped her hands. "Actually, we all have a bit of an advantage over you. We spent a year and a half getting used to Danny being gone. We got letters and phone calls occasionally, but on a day to day basis, we learned to continue with our lives."

Matt reached over and put his hand on her shoulder. "Doesn't make it any easier though, does it?"

She smiled and leaned her cheek onto his hand. "No." She ran her hand over the etched name on the headstone. "I just hope that someday I'm able to find another man as good as he was."

"He would've wanted that," Matt said.

"I know."

"Which brings me to one of the reasons I came to Kansas." He reached behind him and handed Julie the brown sack. "This belongs to you."

Julie set the book in her lap before pulling an envelope out of her purse. "This was in with Danny's personal effects."

Matt took the letter, surprised to see his name written on the outside of the sealed envelope. It was in Danny's chicken scratch. They'd all written letters home in case something happened to them while in the Middle East. Was this what that was?

His hands started to shake. He honestly didn't think he could read it, not now, not in front of Julie and Danny. "Would you mind if I took this with me?" he asked.

Julie shook her head. "It's yours. Do what you need to do with it."

Matt watched as Julie opened the sack and pulled out the album. She immediately put her hand to her mouth as she started to cry. "Danny told me about this," she whispered. She looked up at him. "But you're wrong. It doesn't belong to me, it's yours, and Danny wanted you to have it."

"What?" he asked, his jaw dropping open.

Julie smiled, flipping through the pages. "He told me about the album before he was killed. He said he knew I'd always had specific ideas of how I wanted our wedding, but that he was working on a project with his best friend. He told me it was a way for both of you to think of the future and not the present hell you were both living in."

She looked at him sheepishly. "He told me you were gay and this would probably be your only chance to plan a wedding like this."

Julie turned to the pages filled with flowers. She touched each picture. "I wish I could smell them. Danny wrote about each flower and how each one of them was supposed to smell."

Matt nodded, remembering the stephanotis that Danny was crazy about. He'd heard what Julie had said about the album, but he didn't feel right keeping it. "I'm sorry I took it. I have dreams. Dreams about Danny and flying in that damn Blackhawk and that stupid red book. And the dead. There's always the dead and dying."

Looking up from the pages, Julie seemed to study him for several seconds. "You were in love with him." It wasn't a question, and she didn't seem to be angry, but it still embarrassed him. He turned his head away and gave her a slight nod. He knew he'd never verbally be able to admit it to her.

"I'm glad," Julie said. "It comforts me to know that someone over in that hell hole loved him. He deserved that."

Julie set the book aside and crawled over to wrap her arms around Matt. "Danny hoped one day you'd find some place to settle. Have you?"

"Yeah," Matt said. "A town in Wyoming."

"Is there anyone special waiting for you back home?"

Matt's chin began to quiver. "Yes. Two brilliant doctors who for some reason love me."

"Then go home to them. Build a life for yourself and forget about the past." She reached across the blanket and picked up the album. "Take this with you. It was never meant to be mine."

Matt clutched the book to his chest. "Thank you," he said. He was overwhelmed by her strength and kindness.

Chapter Thirteen

He was so drained it was a wonder he made it back to his hotel. Matt just hoped he was too tired for dreams. The letter in his pocket was a reminder he wasn't finished yet. *Maybe I should wait until I get home to read it.*

He used his key card to get in the side door. The last thing he wanted was another conversation with one of Danny's friends. They seemed to be everywhere, and just then all he wanted was peace.

Matt made it to his room and sat on the edge of the bed. He pulled the letter out of his back pocket and looked at his name scrawled across the front. Could he do it?

The red blinking light on the phone caught his attention. He almost ignored it, he wanted to ignore it, but the thought of an emergency involving his men had him reaching for the phone.

"Front desk."

"This is Matthew Jeffries in room two-fourteen. Do you have a message for me?" he asked Steve.

"Yes. I'm holding a package for you. Would you like me to send it up?"

A package? "Who's it from, does it say?"

"Um, a Dr. Isaac Singer? Do you know this person?" Steve asked.

His heart soared. "Yes, yes, send it up."

Matt hung up the phone. He suddenly felt more awake. Isaac had thought enough to send him something. He wondered what his man had up his sleeve. Knowing Isaac, it was probably something like a plug. He smiled. *Oh that would be so perfect right about now.*

The knock at the door had him digging in his pocket for tip money. He opened the door and took a step back. *Damn, that was some package.* He pulled the six-foot-two package into his room and jumped on him.

Isaac managed to kick the door shut as Matt devoured his mouth. "I can't believe you're here," he said between kisses.

"Sam said you needed me," Isaac returned, and pulled Matt's shirt off over his head.

Matt unbuttoned Isaac's dark brown dress shirt and started on his khaki pants before the statement hit him. "Sam said that?" he asked.

Isaac pushed Matt's pants down and fell to his knees, taking Matt's softening cock into his mouth. Within seconds, Matt's erection was back in full force. He tried to let himself go and just enjoy the incredible blow job Isaac was gifting him with, but thoughts of Sam played in his mind. "Why would Sam say something like that? Isaac?"

Isaac pulled off Matt's cock and led him to the bed. His doctor finished undressing them and lifted the covers back. Matt slid in and waited for an explanation.

His lover wrapped him in a tight embrace, running his hands over Matt's hip. "We had a bit of an argument before I left."

"You and Sam?" *Oh shit, oh shit, oh shit.* "Was it about me?"

"Yes and no. It had a lot to do with my over-active libido." Isaac's hand wandered to run over Matt's ass.

"Is he mad that you're having sex with me?" God, he so did not want to come between these two long-term partners.

Isaac shook his head. "Actually, I think it comes as a bit of a relief to him. It seems all these years he's been afraid if he didn't have sex with me when I wanted, that I'd stray. He's glad that we both have someone to love who can fulfil those desires for me."

"And?" he asked. He knew there had to be more.

"And? I feel like shit for it."

Matt stiffened. His brain told him Isaac had come all this way to let him down in person, but his body was telling him something else. If he were about to get booted to the curb, would Isaac be exploring the crack of his ass?

"Can I ask why you feel like shit for loving me?" he finally asked.

Isaac's brows shot up in surprise. "No. Oh, baby, no." Isaac kissed him, nipping Matt's lips. "We love you. Please don't ever doubt that for a second. I feel like shit that I let my desires cause Sam a moments question about my loyalty to him."

Matt exhaled the breath he hadn't realised he'd been holding. "And Sam?"

"I'm sure if he were here he'd be just as anxious to see you come as I am. He likes sex. He just doesn't desire it as often as the two of us." Isaac pressed his finger against Matt's hole.

"Please tell me you have some lube with you?" Matt asked.

"Are you kidding?" Isaac pulled back and jumped out of bed. He was back within seconds with a brand new bottle of lube in his hand. "They made me throw away what I had in my carry-on. Damn airport security. But I stopped on the way."

Matt grinned. "I would've paid good money to see the security guy confiscating your bottle of lube."

Isaac chuckled as he pushed the covers to the foot of the bed. "Don't think I didn't put up a fight."

He relaxed onto his back and wantonly spread his legs. "I've got a lot to tell you, but I need you to make me forget. Just for a little while." Matt ran his hands over his own nipples, sensitising them.

He watched as a look momentarily flicked over Isaac's face. "What happens when I get to old to get it up?" Isaac asked.

Matt's hand stilled. "Would you love me any less?" he asked.

"No, of course not," Isaac said with a shake of his head.

"There's your answer."

Isaac fell on top of him. "I'm sorry," he said kissing Matt.

Matt opened to Isaac's questing tongue as their cocks rubbed against each other. The longer and deeper the kiss, the tighter his balls became. Matt broke away and looked into the dark brown depths of his lover's eyes. "Make love to me."

Without moving off of him, Isaac popped the cap on the lube and warmed the slick substance between his fingers. "Wanna make you feel good," Isaac said as he introduced a finger to Matt's hole.

Matt's body welcomed the invasion eagerly. "More," he moaned. He wanted to feel it. He needed that bite of pain that only Isaac could give. "I need your cock. Now."

"You're not ready, baby," Isaac soothed pushing another finger inside of Matt.

"I'm past ready. I need it."

Isaac reluctantly removed his fingers and poured a generous amount of lube into his hand. He ran it up and down his length until that beautiful cock was red and shiny. Isaac wiped the excess on Matt's torso with a grin.

Matt felt the tip of his lover's cock at his opening and swung his legs over Isaac's shoulders. "Give it to me. I'm begging you, just do it."

"Shhh," Isaac crooned as he pushed his way inside. "You never have to beg."

Matt felt the momentary sting as his body tried to accept the invasion. "Yessss," he hissed, as Isaac slid home.

"Give me a second," Isaac panted, obviously trying to stave off his orgasm.

Matt reached up and plucked at Isaac's dark brown nipples. His mouth watered as the pebbled nubs hardened even further under his fingers. As responsive as Isaac's body was, Matt doubted there would ever be a time when he lost his lust for sex.

Isaac pulled out and slammed back in, jolting Matt from his musings. "Hell yeah. That's what I'm talking about," Matt shouted.

His lover must have known he needed to get out of his own head, even just for a little while, because after the initial thrust, Matt didn't have time to think. Isaac gripped Matt's shoulders and fucked him like he never had before.

The sounds the two of them made were more animal than human, his lover pegging his gland on every thrust. "Take it," Isaac grunted. "Love this ass," he continued his litany of obscenities as the speed increased.

"Fuck your hand," Isaac commanded.

Matt wrapped his fingers around his throbbing cock. He hadn't dared touch himself, knowing it would only be a matter of moments before he came.

"Shoot that spunk on me, baby. Give it to me," Isaac continued to command.

Matt aimed his cock at Isaac's chest and let loose, spraying his lover with his seed. Rope after rope of the pearly white fluid drenched Isaac's torso.

"Fuck yeah," Isaac grunted and buried himself deep into Matt's ass. Isaac collapsed on Matt as his body shook from the effects of his orgasm.

Matt held on tight as his lover emptied his balls. His head was pounding with the aftermath of his own climax. Damn. He momentarily wondered if he would be able to keep up with Isaac. This must be the way Sam felt. He pushed the worry aside. If he had to take a double dose of vitamins each day to keep up with his man, it would be well worth it.

He unwound his legs from Isaac's shoulders and wrapped them around his love's waist. "That was…"

"Yeah," Isaac agreed.

They lay in each other's arms kissing and exploring. Matt's thoughts drifted. "I miss Sam."

"Me, too," Isaac agreed.

"Let's call the airport and see if we can get an earlier flight home."

Isaac pulled back and looked into Matt's eyes. "Are you sure? Have you done everything here you needed to?"

Matt nodded. "I'm sure I'll still have the occasional nightmare. But with BJ's help and you and Sam in my bed every night, I think I can live with them." He gestured towards the nightstand. "Danny wrote me a letter before he died. Julie gave it to me earlier."

"Have you read it?" Isaac asked.

"No. Maybe someday soon, but I'm not quite ready yet." He realised he was okay with that. For now, it was enough that Danny had thought enough about him to write it in the first place. They'd been told by their commanding officers to write letters for the loved ones they'd be leaving behind should anything happen. The fact that Danny considered him a 'loved one' was all he needed to know for the moment.

Epilogue

One Month Later

Lying beside the pond, with the hot July sun filtering through the leaves, Matt thought about Julie. Their phone call earlier in the day was still on his mind. She sounded happier than she had the last few times they'd talked. Julie confessed that she'd been out on a couple of dates with Rodney. Matt smiled. He'd told her he thought Danny would be pleased and she'd agreed.

He looked over at the two naked men beside him. Despite the heat, they were sound asleep wrapped in each others arms. They'd become his saviours, his everything. They hadn't even taken time to eat the lunch Sam had packed in the cooler. Sometimes their love-making took on a frenzied pace and the minute they'd arrived, they'd shucked their clothes and enveloped each other in passion.

Reaching over, Matt pulled his jeans towards him. He dug in the back pocket and removed the now crumpled and wrinkled letter from his wallet. He'd read the damn thing so many times over the past few weeks, it was in danger of completely falling apart.

Unfolding the single white sheet of paper he held it up with one hand, letting the other fall on Sam's hip.

Dear Matt,

If you're reading this it means I've lost the battle. As long as my body makes it home, I'm okay with it.

If I know you at all, I'm sure you're feeling guilty. I'm right, aren't I? I know because that's the kind of friend you are. Well, if I could see you one last time I'd probably punch you in the nose for it. Stop feeling guilty. We both knew what we were getting into. We both saved a lot of lives by doing what we did. Take pride in that. I do. For every soldier we saved there was one less letter, like this one, going back to the States.

I love you, Matt. I wish I could've felt the same kind of love that you felt for me, but please know my love was no less than if we'd been lovers. Don't ever convince yourself it was wrong, because it wasn't. I'm thankful for every day I had the chance to know you. Now that you've made it home, I want you to forget about the war and focus on yourself. You deserve to find that special someone. If you open yourself enough I have no doubt you'll find it. I wish only the best for you.

Do me a favour and check in on my folks and Julie once in a while. Hopefully I'll be looking down on all of you and not looking up. Ha, Ha.

I'm sure by now you've got the album. Keep it and remember the good times we had together assembling it. It was only ever for you.

I love you, buddy,

Danny

Matt kissed Danny's signature, something he'd gotten into the habit of doing, and refolded the piece of paper.

"You okay?" Sam asked.

He set the letter on top of his jeans and turned to his lover. "Yeah. Why don't you pull yourself away from the human furnace and come over here?" He opened his arms as Sam extradited himself from Isaac's still sleeping body.

Sam snuggled against Matt's chest. "I love you," Sam whispered, licking a path up Matt's neck to his lips.

"I know, and I could never ask for anything more." Matt kissed his lover, comforted in the knowledge that Danny would be twice as happy for him.

"How about I unpack the cooler," Sam said. "Maybe I can get a big piece of Kyle's apple pie before Isaac wakes up."

"I heard that," Isaac grumbled.

In no time Isaac had worked his way between Matt and Sam. Stretched out in the dappled sunlight, Isaac was magnificent. Matt looked at Sam and winked. "How 'bout we use Isaac as a plate?"

Sam licked his lips. "That's the best idea I've heard all day."

"Eat away," Isaac said and raised his arms over his head.

OUT OF THE
SHADOW

Dedication

To those of us who try in vain to live up to others expectations, only to find that someone else's life is not the one we're meant to live.

Chapter One

"Hey, boss. You want to sign off on this list of stock for the Rodeo Days?"

Shep looked over the top of his tiny reading glasses. He'd been trying to figure out where he'd screwed up the books, and damned if he could find it. "You've got a list together already?"

Rance grinned and tilted the white straw hat up higher on his forehead. "It's the beginning of June. We barely have a month before the rodeo."

Shep looked down at his desk calendar. "Damn. Where the hell has the time gone?" He took the list from Rance and glanced over it. "Looks good. You sure about Tabasco Red?"

"He'll be ready. Jeremy's been working with him."

"Jeremy?" Shep stood and put his hands on his hips. "You trying to get me sued? That boy'll fall off and break his damn neck." An image of the lean dark haired boy lying on the ground twisted and broken, caused an ache in his gut.

Rance chuckled and shook his head. "You haven't been paying enough attention lately. Jeremy is the best bull rider we've got."

Shep narrowed his eyes and gave a mock growl.

"Well, except for you that is." Rance quickly amended with a cheeky grin. "He's not a boy anymore either. Why he's working here instead of out on the circuit I'll never understand. You'd think with his connections he could write his own ticket on the pro tour."

Shep sat back down and handed the list to Rance. "He has his reasons I'm sure. The list looks fine."

Rance nodded and started to walk out of Shep's home office. "Rance," he called after the cowboy.

Rance turned. "Good job," Shep said with a nod of approval.

"Thanks," Rance said and continued out the door.

After his foreman left, Shep tried to go back to his books, but thoughts of Jeremy kept filtering through his mind. He'd always thought Jeremy chose to live at the Back Breaker because of his sexual orientation. Life must be hard enough being the son of the reigning world champion. To be the *gay* son of the same man would be intolerable out on the Professional Bull Riders circuit. Shep knew what it was like. He'd lived the life for years, always afraid he'd misstep and out himself.

He took off his glasses and tossed them to the old scarred desk. He was forced into retirement once Devil's Due had tossed and then trampled him. Building the ranch seemed like the logical thing to do at the time. Shep chuckled to himself. *I thought my lonely days were over.*

Shaking his head, he reached for his glasses once more. He'd loved to look at the young slim cowboys on the tour. It was his hope that being the boss of his own ranch would make him feel like a kid in a candy store. And he had been that kid, for a couple of years at least. He'd discreetly indulged himself in the bow legged men as they filtered in and out of his employment. Until…

"Boss!" Rance shouted, running back into his office. "I think you should come out here."

Shep stood and was already on his way out the door before he'd even given Rance a chance to tell him what was wrong. In this business, seconds mattered. A slow response time could mean the difference between life and death. "What's up?" he asked, opening the front door.

"When I left your office, I noticed Jeremy's truck parked out back. I went to the bunkhouse to see how his trip up to see his dad went and found him in bed." Rance reached out and grabbed Shep's arm, pulling him to a stop.

"He's been beat up, Boss." Rance motioned to his face. "He's holding a bloodied rag over his cheek. I think we might need to get him to town."

"Shit," Shep spat out and raced towards the bunkhouse. His chest tightened as he threw open the door to the room Jeremy shared with the new hired hand, Bo. Luckily, Bo was out in the hayfield. It would've been hard for the kind-hearted man not to try and help had he been present.

He stepped into the room and went immediately to one knee beside Jeremy's bunk. Rance was a little off in his assessment of Jeremy. He hadn't been beaten, merely hit once it appeared. The left side of Jeremy's sweet face was bruised and swollen from what he could see under the bloody rag. "Let me see it," Shep commanded as he reached for the cloth.

"I'm fine," Jeremy mumbled. "Just opened my mouth when I shouldn't have."

"I'll be the judge as to whether or not you're fine," Shep said. He covered Jeremy's long fingered hand with his own and forcibly lifted the rag from his face. The cut was still open and about an inch and a half long, but because it was on his cheekbone, Shep knew it needed stitches.

"I'm taking you to see one of the docs. Are you going to come willingly, or will I have to carry you like a child?" He hated talking that way to Jeremy, but knew the boy was as stubborn as his father. He should know. Todd Lovell had been his best friend for the past twelve years, and a more stubborn man you'd never meet.

Jeremy looked at him and grunted. "I'm not a child."

"Then don't act like one, and get your ass into my truck." Shep held out a hand and turned back to look at Rance. "Bring my truck around, will ya?"

His foreman nodded and left, just as Jeremy took hold of Shep's hand. Shep gave a slight tug and got the boy to his feet. The movement put Jeremy's lean body against his. With a stuttered breath, Shep took a step back. No sense in making a fool of himself when Jeremy, more than anyone, was off limits.

"Let me get you a clean washcloth," he said. He quickly made his way down the hall to the small shelf in the bathroom. By the time he'd wet the rag, Jeremy was leaning against the door jamb.

He turned around and once again came face to face with Jeremy. "Here." Shep took the bloodied rag out of Jeremy's hand and replaced it with the clean one. A honking horn alerted him that Rance was back with his truck.

He gestured towards the hall. "Let's go." He waited for Jeremy to turn and start walking towards the front door before following at a discreet distance.

Once in the truck and headed for town, Shep cleared his throat. "Gonna tell me who did this?"

"Nope," Jeremy said, refusing to look away from the passenger window.

Shep wondered if Jeremy opened his mouth and came on to the wrong cowboy. One thing he could say for Jeremy, the boy didn't seem to be embarrassed by his sexual desires for other men. It wasn't that he acted proud of the fact that he was gay, Jeremy just never had tried to hide it. Most likely it's what had gotten him into trouble. Shep would think the kid would've learned by now that the rodeo circuit wasn't the place to cruise for dates.

He remembered the first time he'd met Jeremy. He'd guess it had been about five years since that day. Shep was sharing a fifth-wheel trailer with Todd when his best friend had received the call that his ex-wife had died in an automobile accident. Todd had left immediately and returned three days later with Jeremy.

At seventeen, Jeremy Lovell had moved in with them. His immediate announcement to his father that he was gay and had come out to his mother two years prior came as a shock. As the days turned to weeks, Shep knew he had to part company with his best friend, or go to jail. Jeremy had been too much temptation to bear.

He'd been thinking of Jeremy and his inappropriate desires for the young man, the day he was almost killed by Devil's Due. A small part of him was relieved that he could use the career-ending injury to his knee and hip as an excuse to get away from Jeremy.

The ranch suited his needs for the next four years until Jeremy showed up on his doorstep, duffle slung over his shoulder. Shep had been handed a note from Todd that would change his life forever.

Shep,

Please take care of Jeremy for me. My life on the circuit is not right for him. You of all people know how dangerous it can be for an openly gay man. I fear that Jeremy will be found dead behind a stock trailer one day, and I can no longer sit by and do nothing to protect my son. If our friendship ever meant anything to you, I pray that you will give him a job and a home.

Your friend,

Todd

Shep had had no choice but to welcome Jeremy into his ranch family. He knew he should've allowed Jeremy the use of one of his guest rooms in the large ranch house, but he also knew what would come of it. It had been hard enough to keep his distance from the younger man with him living in the bunkhouse with the rest of the cowboys, but so far he'd done it. He would continue to hold fast to his promise to Todd to protect Jeremy, even if it was from himself.

Pulling up in front of the clinic, Shep parked and helped Jeremy out of the truck. Sam Browning met them at the emergency entrance. "Yep. Looks like you've got a nasty cut," Sam said ushering them inside.

Sam handed Shep a clipboard and pen. "Why don't you fill these out while I get Jeremy stitched up."

"I'll need your wallet," Shep said to Jeremy.

Jeremy dug into his back pocket and withdrew the cracked leather wallet. "Insurance card is in the front," Jeremy said, as Sam led him to an exam room.

Taking a seat, Shep started filling in the form, name, address, and as much as he knew about Jeremy's medical history. He opened the wallet and found the insurance card. After copying down the information, he slipped the card back in its designated slot.

He smiled at the obvious round ring pressed into the soft leather. At least he'd taught the boy enough to carry protection at all times. The pain he felt over Jeremy fucking some nameless cowboy surprised him.

Knowing he shouldn't, his curiosity got the better of him and he nosed through the rest of the wallet. He found a picture of Jeremy's mother tucked between the folds and pulled it out. When he did so, another picture fluttered to the floor at his feet. He bent to retrieve it and stopped. It was a picture of him and Jeremy taken about four years ago on the boy's eighteenth birthday.

Shep willed his fingers to work. He slowly picked up the fallen photo. He remembered the picture well because he had one just like it in his photo album at the ranch. Jeremy's had been altered though to cut his father out of the frame. Shep wondered if he'd cropped it so it would fit into his wallet. Yes. He was sure that had been the reason, though he refused to let himself wonder why he'd kept Shep's face in the picture and not his own father's.

Quickly stuffing the pictures back to their hiding place, Shep finished the rest of the form. With the clipboard in hand, he went in search of Doc and Jeremy. He found them in the first exam room. "There are a few medical questions I can't answer," he said.

"Okay," Jeremy said, wincing as Sam gave him a deadening shot directly into the wound.

Shep poised the pen above the paper. As he read down the list, he checked them off one by one as Jeremy answered. "Any broken bones?" he asked as he came to the next question.

When Jeremy didn't answer right away, Shep looked up from his paper. "Jeremy?"

"A broken arm when I was fourteen," Jeremy actually grinned. "I got that falling off a mechanical bull. And two broken ribs a couple of years ago."

Shep's pen still hovered above the paper. "How did you break your ribs? I don't remember hearing about that." He knew it had to have been about a year before Jeremy had come to live at the ranch.

"Fight." Jeremy turned his head.

Shep could tell he wouldn't get anything further out of him. "Okay. So why don't you tell me what you were doing on a mechanical bull?"

"Training," Jeremy mumbled. "I was a naïve kid. I thought if I learned to ride bulls like the old man, he'd finally take an interest in me." Jeremy chuckled, but it wasn't out of happiness. "I was a fool."

He wanted to question Jeremy's response but thought better of it. Pushing the younger man to reveal anything was like butting your head against a brick wall. Shep decided to let the comment drop for now.

Going back to the task at hand, Shep finished filling out the form with Jeremy's help as Sam stitched him up. He foolishly hoped Jeremy's tongue would loosen after Doc gave him the pain medicine Shep was sure would come.

Chapter Two

By the time Shep got Jeremy home and in his bunk it was getting dark. He gave Bo strict instructions to come and get him if Jeremy's cheek started bleeding through the bandage. Thankfully Bo knew better than to touch the boy. The new hired hand had been upfront about his HIV status before Shep had even agreed to hire him. Knowing what he did, Shep didn't see a problem with Bo's medical condition as long as he was mindful.

He said a quick goodnight to the cowboys, and went back to the main house. As soon as he got in, he went to his office and picked up the phone. He knew Todd rode earlier, which was the reason for Jeremy's trip, but he didn't know if Todd knew of the apparent fight his son had been in.

"Hello," Todd slurred just a bit.

"You been out drinking, old man?" Shep chuckled.

"Just a bit," Todd replied.

"Well, I hope it was celebratory and not drowning your sorrows."

"Hell, you know me better than that. Of course it was celebratory. How the hell are ya?"

"Good," Shep said. "Listen, Jeremy came back home earlier with a nasty cut on his cheek…"

"I had nothin' to do with it," Todd said, cutting Shep off.

That's weird. "Didn't say that you did. I just thought I'd call in case you didn't know where he was." Something just didn't feel right. "Do you know who did it?"

"Nope," Todd answered.

Shep could feel his anger rising with his old friend. He wasn't sure if it was the alcohol, or if he'd interrupted Todd with one of the buckle bunnies that always hung around. Regardless, the lack of concern for his own son shocked him.

"Call me when you're sober," Shep said and hung up. Knowing Todd was likely to call back and pick a fight, Shep took the phone off the hook and left the office.

* * * *

Walking out to the barn three days later, Shep's attention was diverted to the small indoor arena. A crowd of cowboys had gathered, for what appeared to be a test run of one of his bulls. Changing directions, he walked into the dimly lit building.

What he saw nearly stopped his heart. There was Jeremy atop Tabasco Red, being flung around the ring like a rag doll. Shep wanted to leap the fence and strangle him. Instead he waited the full eight seconds.

Once Jeremy was safely out of harm's way, he blew his stack. "Jeremy! In my office, NOW!" He turned on his heels and stalked back to the house. His heart was still beating a mile a minute when Jeremy knocked on the door jam.

Shep gestured to one of the chairs in front of his desk. He still didn't trust himself to speak for fear of yelling his head off. For three days he'd done his damndest to not hover over Jeremy. He figured the last thing the kid would want was mothering by an old broken down rodeo guy.

"Did I do something wrong?" Jeremy asked.

"You could say that." Shep took off his straw hat and tossed it to the credenza behind him. "You still taking pain meds?"

Jeremy shook his head. "Not since that first night."

That was something at least. "What were you thinking getting on that bull with your face only starting to heal? You trying to bust open the stitches? Cuz you were damn lucky that didn't happen."

He watched as Jeremy's spine stiffened. "I know what I'm doing on the back of a bull. I'm not one of your greenhorns."

"You're only twenty-two fucking years old," Shep yelled, his blood pressure on the rise again.

Jeremy flinched like Shep had struck him. He slowly stood and fit his hat back on his dark brown hair. "Are you gonna fire me for doing my job?"

"Since when is trying to get yourself killed in your job description?" Shep asked.

Jeremy looked down at the floor. "Since Rance told me to make sure Red was ready for the rodeo." Jeremy closed his eyes and shook his head. "Red's not the first bull I've taken for a test drive. Maybe if you'd stop thinking of me as a kid, you'd see that I'm damn good at my job."

Shep opened his mouth to say something before promptly closing it. Was Jeremy right? He'd admit to himself that he hadn't paid attention to what Jeremy did on the ranch. It had taken a lot of willpower over the previous year to even be on the same five hundred acres as the slim cowboy, and not jump his bones. He'd purposely not sought Jeremy out for just that reason.

"If there's nothing else, I have work I need to get back to," Jeremy said. The younger man was smart enough to wait for Shep to dismiss him.

He finally nodded. "Stay off the livestock until your face heals completely. I'm sure Rance can find something else for you to do in the meantime."

"Yes, sir."

"Sir? Since when do you call me sir?" Shep asked. He hated to admit it, but it hurt hearing Jeremy talk to him like he was nothing but a boss.

"Since I showed up on your doorstep, and you started treating me like a stranger, I reckon."

Shep saw two things. The obvious hurt in Jeremy's big brown eyes and the tick of his jaw as he clenched his teeth. "You're right," Shep admitted. "I didn't want you to have trouble with the other hands by showing you special treatment. Guess I went overboard." He didn't dare confess the real reason he'd kept Jeremy at arm's length.

Jeremy started to leave but stopped. He didn't turn around, but Shep heard the words loud and clear. "You're all I have left," Jeremy said right before he walked out the door.

The softly spoken words took any remaining anger Shep had held on to. He slumped back in his chair and ran his scarred, rough hands over his face. "You're all I have left," he whispered the words aloud.

What the hell was going on between Todd and his son? He vowed to drop a few of the barriers he'd erected and get reacquainted with his young ranch hand. Young. That was the key word for Shep. Jeremy was seventeen years his junior. At twenty-two, Jeremy may be of legal age, but he still had a lot of oats to sow, and when, or if, Shep ever admitted his feelings, Jeremy would be his. He had no plans to share and would never forgive someone who fucked around behind his back.

He only hoped he could at least stay in the young man's good graces until the time was right. Shep vowed to take a greater interest in Jeremy's talents that his foreman spoke of.

He studied the phone in front of him, three days and still no call from Todd. Jeremy's words came back to him once more. What was Jeremy trying to tell him, that he no longer had a father?

Todd had never had a problem with Shep's sexual preferences, at least none that he'd ever voiced. Did his old friend feel differently because Jeremy was his son? Is that why he didn't seem overly concerned about his son's injury?

Looking at the clock, he was surprised the morning had already slipped by. If he didn't get a move on, he'd miss lunch. He could always make himself a sandwich in his own kitchen, but lunch with the guys sounded preferable to a meal alone.

With one last glance at the phone, Shep picked up his hat and settled it on his head. Surely he could show Jeremy he still cared without giving away just how much.

By the time he walked into the bunkhouse, his brow was already perspiring. He hung his hat on the peg just inside the door and wiped his forehead with the bandana he always kept in his pocket.

After taking a seat, he was pleased to see Jeremy enter and hang his hat next to Shep's. He actually smiled when the younger man pulled the bright red square of cloth from his pocket and wiped his own brow and neck. "I've taught you well," he chuckled.

Jeremy's head snapped up. Evidently he was unaware of Shep's presence at the long kitchen table. "Slumming it today?" Jeremy asked, taking a seat several chairs away from Shep.

Not about to be baited into an argument, Shep simply slid over until he was next to Jeremy. "Felt the need for something other than a sandwich."

No one but his cook, Frank, was in the room. Taking a chance, Shep gestured towards Jeremy's bandaged cheek. "You been watching it for infection?"

Jeremy nodded, and filled a glass with iced tea from the pitcher on the table. "You mind if I take a look?" Shep asked. He knew he was pushing his luck, but no pain, no gain.

Reaching up, Jeremy pealed the bandage back, exposing the healing cut. The skin around the sutures was still a livid purple, making Shep automatically wince. "Looks sore. Are you sure you don't need anything for the pain?"

"I'm sure," Jeremy said. "The pills made me too tired. I can't work if I take them."

"You've worked non-stop for over a year. I'd say you're due some days off if you need them."

The young cowboy shook his head. "Naw, I'm fine," he said, playing nervously with his silverware.

Shep could tell there was something else Jeremy wanted to say. He covered the younger man's hand with his own, stilling the tinkling of the fork and knife. "Tell me what's on your mind."

Jeremy turned to look at Shep briefly before looking down at their touching hands. "I'm damn good at the bulls. It's what gets me up in the morning. If you take that away…"

God, Jeremy sounded so much like him in his younger days. If he was as good as he said, why was he working the ranch instead of out earning prize money? "I won't take it away. But you really do need to let that cut heal first."

"Why? I seem to recall plenty of times when you got back on a bull even though you'd been injured. Why is this any different?"

Shep squeezed Jeremy's hand slightly. "Because I was stupid. I didn't have anyone who cared enough to stop me."

Jeremy turned his head and looked directly into Shep's eyes. "I didn't think you'd listen to me."

He grinned. "I probably wouldn't have. But maybe if I had, I'd still be riding." His hand automatically went to his scarred knee. He was luckier than most, because his injuries only bothered him when it was damp outside. Shep knew of other cowboys who were either dead or damn near invalids, after getting stomped and thrown around by a sixteen hundred pound bull. Jeremy's words began to sink in. Was the younger man trying to tell him that he'd cared enough to try and stop him back in the day? Something in his chest shifted.

The door flew open and in poured four more hungry cowboys. Shep released Jeremy's hand and smiled at his employees. "Hot enough for you outside?" he asked with a grin.

Rance took his hat off and straddled the chair across the table from Shep. "Jeremy tells me I have to find something else for him to do for a while."

He started to automatically confirm the need for a safer job, but stopped himself. He looked at Jeremy before turning back to Rance. "I don't care if he works with the bulls, but no riding for a few more days. If you have one you need to test out, come get me."

Rance's eyes went wide. "Seriously? I haven't seen you on the back of a bull in almost two years."

Shep chuckled. "Like riding a bike."

Jeremy shifted in his seat. "Some of the bulls are pretty nasty to deal with, Shep."

For some reason the comment smacked at Shep's pride. He narrowed his eyes, staring down the younger man. "Can you stay on 'em?"

He watched as Jeremy's Adam's apple bobbed. "Yeah."

Shep gave a profound nod. "There's only one person at this table who used to ride professionally." Even while saying it, Shep knew he was coming off as a conceited ass, but damn. Did Jeremy see him as an old broken down man? Hell, the boy was only seventeen years younger.

Jeremy broke eye contact first. He pushed away from the table and stood. "I think I'll take Bo some lunch out in the hayfield."

Shep noticed the look Rance gave Jeremy before nodding. "I think he's out in the east pasture."

Jeremy nodded and walked into the kitchen. He was back a moment later with a smaller cooler in hand. He took his hat from the peg and settled it on his head. "I won't be long. I know we're video taping the yearlings later."

As soon as Jeremy was out the door, Rance reached across the table and punched Shep in the shoulder. "Since when do you get into pissing contests with twenty year olds?"

"He's twenty-two," Shep corrected his foreman. "And I didn't like the way he made it sound like I was too old to ride."

Rance's handsome face broke out into a grin. "So it's like that is it?"

Damn, he should've known he couldn't keep anything from his foreman. Rance could read people better than anyone he'd ever met. Shep knew his secret was out, but at least it took his friend a year to realise it. "Shut up," he said, and took a good natured swipe at his foreman.

Rance held up his hands in mock surrender. "I won't say a word."

Chapter Three

As he crested the hill, Jeremy spotted the billowing dust kicked up by the mower. It looked like Bo was making good progress. He knew by the end of the week, the field would be baled into tight round bundles of hay.

He drove the ranch truck as close to the tractor as he dared and honked the horn. Bo waved an acknowledgement and finished the strip he was on before shutting down the old John Deer.

"Lunch," Jeremy yelled, holding up the cooler.

Bo walked across the field smiling. "You must've read my mind."

Jeremy let down the truck's tailgate and took a seat. He opened the cooler and dug out two sandwiches, handing one to Bo as soon as he settled next to him. "There's another in there for you, too."

"Thanks," Bo said, taking a big bite. "So...why the unexpected delivery? Not that I don't appreciate it, but you've never brought me lunch before."

Jeremy shrugged. "Just needed to get away for a few minutes."

Bo nodded and took another bite. "Away from the ranch or the boss?"

"I should've never told you about my feelings for Shep." Looking at his sandwich, he suddenly lost his appetite. "Here, you want this?" he asked.

"You need to eat it," Bo answered. "Besides, you didn't exactly tell me about Shep if you remember."

Jeremy felt his face heat. No. He hadn't told his roommate about his feelings. He'd had the misfortune of calling out Shep's name while jacking off one night. He thought everyone else was in town, but Bo had surprised him by walking into the bedroom at that precise moment.

He tried to take another bite of the ham and cheese sandwich, but it felt like sawdust in his throat. "Doesn't matter," he said, putting the remains of his lunch back into the small plastic bag. "He sees me as a kid. Always has and always will."

"You might be surprised at what Shep sees when he looks at you." Bo fished into the cooler and came back with a can of iced tea and a second sandwich.

"Why do you say that?"

Bo shrugged. "Just a feeling. I mean, you gotta know you're hot. I doubt there's a cowboy on the ranch that hasn't thought of getting into those skin tight Wranglers."

He couldn't help but to smile. Yeah, he'd noticed several of the guys checking his ass a time or two, but no one interested him but Shep. Sure, he indulged in the occasional slap and tickle between stock trailers while he lived with his dad, but he knew he needed to learn. The last thing he wanted was to make a fool of himself if he ever got Shep in the position to show him how much he loved and wanted him. He was still no expert, but he'd learned quite a few tricks from the closeted cowboys on the circuit.

Feeling a little better, he dug out a bag of chips. He and Bo ate in a comfortable silence for several minutes, before Bo had to ruin it.

"Are you ever going to tell me who decked ya?"

His spine stiffened. He'd been threatened to not breathe a word of his attacker's name. Still, he'd carried the burden for so long…

"Let's just say I won't be going to visit my father again. Ever." *Shit.* He could tell by the look on Bo's face he knew exactly what had happened. Jeremy wondered what kind of fallout he'd have to suffer if his old man found out he'd been talking.

"You can't say anything to anyone," Jeremy quickly added.

Bo tossed the empty can in the bed of the truck. "That's fucked up."

"Yeah," Jeremy agreed.

"Why'd he do it?" Bo asked.

Jeremy could see the corded muscles in Bo's arms flex with unleashed anger. "I told him I was thinking about entering the Cattle Valley Rodeo."

Bo jumped off the tailgate and spun to face Jeremy head on. "What? He hit you because you wanted to compete in a damn rodeo? Doesn't he know how good you are?"

Jeremy chuckled. "Yeah, he does. That's the problem."

His friend started pacing back and forth over the mowed hay. "I don't get it," Bo finally said.

Neither do I. He'd tried to figure his dad out for years. He'd spent his entire childhood looking up to the man. Hell, he'd worked his ass off trying to learn to ride bulls just to please his estranged father.

"When I was twenty, I entered a competition without telling my dad. For years I'd practiced behind his back. I wanted to wait until I knew I was good enough to earn his respect. I'd managed to save enough for the entry fee and thought it would be a good surprise for him. I wanted him to know that I wanted to be just like him." Jeremy stopped, remembering that day brought nothing but heartache.

He shrugged his shoulders. "Anyway, that was the last competition I ever entered."

Bo didn't say anything for several moments. "Well, I know you're damn good. I've seen you with my own eyes, so I reckon you were a little too good for the World Champion Todd Lovell to handle."

"Something like that." Jeremy got out another can of tea and passed it to Bo before closing the cooler. He jumped off the tailgate. "I'd better be getting back."

Bo reached out and touched Jeremy's arm. "If you ask Shep, he'll help you win the competition."

Jeremy shook his head. "It's not worth losing my father completely." Despite everything, he still loved his dad. He may not hold much respect for the man or even like him, but he was still the only real family he had left.

"Seems to me, your dad has done that all on his own. Maybe it's time you stood up for yourself."

Jeremy thought about what Bo had said all the way back to the ranch. What would his dad do to him if he entered? He fingered the bandage on his face.

* * * *

"Do me a favour and take this up to Shep," Rance said, handing Jeremy the tape they'd shot of the yearling bulls and heifers.

"Why me?" Jeremy asked. He hadn't seen Shep since he'd walked out of the bunkhouse earlier in the day.

"Well, number one because I'm your boss and told you to. And number two, because I'm going into town to meet with the celebration committee."

He looked at the tape in Rance's hand and eventually took it from him. Jeremy looked down at himself. "Mind if I get a shower first? I think I have more cow shit and dust on me than skin."

Rance smiled. "Whatever, pretty boy. Just make sure Shep gets that."

Jeremy took a quick shower and put on a clean pair of jeans and a white muscle shirt. Due to the heat, he was tempted to put on a pair of shorts but refrained. Real cowboys didn't wear shorts. He did forgo his boots for a pair of flip flops though.

Snatching the tape of the corner off his dresser, he passed Bo in the hall. "I'll be back in a few if you feel like a game of cards," Jeremy said.

"Sounds good," Bo replied. "Where are you off to?"

He held up the tape. "Rance asked me to deliver this to Shep."

"Ask him about training you while you're there," Bo said as he continued walking to their room.

Jeremy had thought about it all afternoon. Would Shep help him? Maybe it would be a good way of spending time with the object of his desire. By the time he knocked on the door, he'd made his mind up. Some things were more important than stroking your old man's ego.

The door opened and Shep stood in front of him in nothing but a pair of jeans. Jeremy's heart started pounding in his chest. It had been a long time since he'd seen Shep without a shirt. Despite the small amount of grey mixed in with his usual black chest hair, he looked the same. Shep's body was still as hard and sculpted as the first time he'd laid eyes on him.

Shep cleared his throat, and Jeremy's gaze wandered up to the bluest eyes he'd ever seen. Flustered at getting caught ogling his boss, he held out the video. "Rance asked me to drop this by."

"Thanks," Shep said and reached for the tape. Their fingers brushed and if it wasn't his imagination, Shep took a few extra seconds to retrieve the object from his hand.

Before Shep could shut the door, Jeremy spoke again. "I was wondering if you had a few minutes? I'd like to ask you about something." He wasn't sure if the fluttering in his stomach was nerves, or more likely, standing so close to an almost naked Shep.

"Sure," Shep said, taking a step back and gesturing towards the interior of the house.

Jeremy stepped in and Shep shut the door. "Should we go into the office, or would you rather join me for a beer in the kitchen?"

"Beer sounds good." Maybe it would help calm his nerves. He followed Shep's jean encased ass to the kitchen. Lord have mercy, the older man had a nice butt. When Shep bent over to dig in the fridge, it was all Jeremy could do not to moan. He barely caught himself before Shep turned around.

"Make yourself at home." Shep turned one of the chairs around and straddled the seat. Jeremy's mouth watered at the way Shep's heavily muscled forearms rested on the back of it.

He was so fucking hard, he quickly took a seat. He just hoped like hell that Shep hadn't noticed his reaction before he got it hidden under the table. After popping the top on the can of beer, he took a long swallow, gathering his nerve.

"I want to enter the Cattle Valley Rodeo, and I want you to help me win," he finally blurted out.

Shep looked surprised at first, but quickly narrowed his eyes. "You ever competed?"

"Once," Jeremy admitted.

"And how did you do?"

Jeremy shrugged. "I only rode one round. Made it the whole eight seconds though and got a damn good score."

Shep's head tilted to the side as he seemed to study Jeremy. "Why only one round?"

He wasn't about to confess what had really happened that day. "Got into a fight and broke my ribs before round two."

Shep actually grinned. "Feeling a little too cocky and spouting off were you?"

Jeremy felt his gut clench. "Something like that."

Shep drained his beer. "Why ask me and not your dad? He's a hell of a lot better than I am."

"Because I don't want him to know," Jeremy answered. "Please tell me that you won't spill the beans."

Chuckling, Shep shook his head and retrieved another beer from the fridge. "I won't say a word. It's your surprise." He held the new can up. "You ready for another?"

Jeremy lifted the half empty can to his mouth and drained it. "Sure." He wasn't used to drinking, so he told himself he'd only have one more. Honestly, he shouldn't even have accepted the first one. He'd been so sore after working with the yearlings, that he'd taken one of his pain pills. Still, he couldn't bring himself to turn down a beer. It had been a long time since he'd had such a nice conversation with Shep.

"If you feel up to it, we could watch some old tapes of me riding. I could maybe point out a few tricks that I learned throughout my career," Shep offered.

Jeremy smiled and nodded. "I'd like that."

They moved to the den, and Jeremy took a seat on the deep leather couch. Shep popped an old VCR tape into the antique looking video deck and turned it on. "I'll be right back."

Shep was only gone a moment when he returned with two more beers. "This way I don't have to get up in the middle."

Jeremy took the can and set it beside him on the end table. He settled in to watch snippets of Shep's past performances. Shep may talk about Todd being a better rider, but Shep was a genuine showman. Jeremy saw the differences in their style right away. He wondered how his dad had felt about his best friend being better than he was.

"If you hadn't gotten hurt, I bet you would've been world champion by now," Jeremy commented.

When he got no reaction from Shep he looked over to where the man was sitting. Shep had a faraway look on his face. "Shep?"

"It just wasn't meant to be," Shep finally said.

"Did you and my dad fight much back then?" He knew he was asking a question that wasn't any of his business, but he needed to know. Was his father mean to all his competition, or just his son?

Shep drained his beer and opened another can. "We had disagreements. Mostly because of me being gay. Your dad never said it, but I think it worried him having an openly gay son living in the same small trailer with a closeted gay man."

Huh? "You weren't out on the circuit? Why don't I remember that? You were always open at home with the fact that you preferred male company."

"It just wasn't done. Hell, it's still not done. There are plenty of gay men who ride, but very few who have the balls to admit it."

"And you didn't have the balls? I find that hard to believe." Jeremy caught himself looking directly at the bulge in Shep's tight jeans. Oh yeah, Shep definitely had the balls.

"That's what your dad and I fought over. He said he couldn't room with me anymore if I came out to the other riders. He didn't want people to think he was a fag." Shep ran his hand through his salt and pepper hair. "I cared more about his friendship than coming out, so I kept my activities to dark alleys and strange motel rooms."

The way he said it, Jeremy could tell it still left a bitter taste in Shep's mouth. It made him wonder why he'd put up with such a one-sided friendship for so long. "Were you in love with my dad?" he asked.

"No." Shep shook his head vehemently. "Todd was definitely not my type."

Jeremy finished his beer and opened the next. "What exactly is, or was, your type?"

Shep started to say something, but snapped his mouth shut. "My business."

He hadn't meant to make Shep mad. "Fair enough. Sorry I asked."

They both turned to watch the television. Not much was said after that, but occasionally Shep would point out a particular arm position.

After his third beer, Jeremy's eyes started drifting shut. The next thing he knew, Shep was sitting beside him on the couch, with a hand on his chest.

"Wake up, sleepyhead."

Jeremy opened his eyes to stare into the blue depths of Shep's. "Sorry. Did I fall asleep on ya?"

"Not on me, no," Shep chuckled and then coughed. "You always did have a tendency to fall asleep in front of the TV." He motioned towards the stairs. "If you want, there's a spare room upstairs."

The thought of sleeping down the hall from Shep hardened his cock. No way could he behave himself, especially not with the beer and pain pill combination he'd consumed. He shook his head and sat up. "That's okay. I wouldn't want Bo to get the wrong idea."

He watched as Shep's jaw ticked. "You got something going with him? I told you when you agreed to room with him that he's HIV positive."

Jeremy looked down at Shep's hand still pressed against his chest. "No. Bo and I are just friends. It was more your reputation as a hard ass boss I was thinking of."

Shep looked down at his hand and immediately removed it and stood. "Sorry. None of my business."

Jeremy stood and smoothed down his muscle shirt that had ridden up. "Will you still help me with the training?"

"Yeah. If you agree to do it my way."

Jeremy nodded his agreement.

"We'll start training every night for a couple of hours after supper." Shep stuffed his hands in his front pockets.

"Okay. Thanks." Jeremy walked towards the front door. "I had a nice evening. Thanks for the beer."

"You're welcome. See you later."

Jeremy walked back to the bunkhouse more confused than ever. Was Shep mad because he'd fallen asleep? He'd seemed different when he woke up.

Chapter Four

The following morning, Shep was in a pissy mood. He'd barely gotten a wink of sleep and his cock felt raw. Jeremy's skin haunted his dreams. Twice during the night and once before bed, he'd jerked off remembering the smooth expanse of skin left visible when the younger man's shirt had worked up in sleep.

They'd been watching the tape when Shep turned to tell Jeremy something and found the other man sound asleep, slumped sideways on the couch. He'd smiled and walked over to try and rouse him, but the sight of all that sun-bronzed skin had mesmerised him.

The next thing he knew, he was sitting on the couch hip to hip with Jeremy. As gorgeous as Jeremy was when he was awake, he was even more so asleep. Those long black lashes fanned over the sharp cheekbones in an almost feminine fashion. Shep longed to run his tongue over Jeremy's thin upper lip and fuller bottom lip. Even more he wanted to delve inside to taste the man he'd fantasised about for years.

By the time he finished his oatmeal, thoughts of Jeremy had him hard once more. Dammit. He was going to have to do something about this situation. No way would he be able to work closely with the younger man with a woody in his jeans the entire time.

A knock on the screen door made him jump. "Come on in," he said gruffly.

Rance stuck his head in the door. "Just wanted to make sure you got that tape."

"Yeah, I got it. Haven't had a chance to look at it though. Any prospects in the bunch?" Talking to Rance about business started to deflate his cock. "Come on in and grab a cup of coffee."

Rance stepped into the kitchen and pulled his customary cup from the cupboard. "There were two that showed signs of being damn fine rodeo stock, so I don't think I'll be bucking them again any time soon. Couple more I don't want to cull from the prospects list. I'll give them another six months and try 'em again with just the flank."

Shep nodded and took a sip of his coffee. "I trust your judgement."

"Thanks," Rance said. He didn't sit at the table with Shep, instead choosing to lean against the counter. "Jeremy mentioned that you were going to work with him after supper."

"Yep. If he wants to win, he'll need to work his ass off in order to be ready in time."

"Which bull do you want me to get ready?"

"None for now. I'm going to make him go back to the beginning and use the old mechanical that I have in the back of the barn."

Rance's black brows shot up. "I didn't know that old thing even worked."

"It don't. That's my project for the day. It just needs a motor, but I should be able to get that in Sheridan before lunch."

Rance chuckled and shook his head. "He's not gonna like it."

"I don't much care. Until I've seen his skill level for myself, I'm not putting him on top of a fourteen to sixteen hundred pound bull. Besides, it's a lot easier to teach when you can actually stand beside the rider and help position his arm."

"Mmm hmm, I just bet you're interested in the position of Jeremy's arm."

"Shut up," Shep grumbled. *Damn.* Rance was going to give him shit every damn day now that he'd figured out his feelings for Jeremy.

Finished with his coffee, Rance rinsed his cup and put it back in the cupboard. "You know more about showboating than me. I'll leave it to the master," Rance said with a mock bow.

Laughing, Shep threw his wadded up napkin at his foreman. "Get out of here and go find some work to do."

"I'm goin'." Rance let the door close behind him before cracking another joke through the screen. "I'll make sure and keep the rest of the hands out of the barn while you and Jeremy train." Rance strode off, laughing himself silly.

Shep shook his head, but couldn't help the small chuckle that escaped. "Jack ass."

* * * *

"Fuck. Are you even listening to me?" Shep blew out a frustrated sigh and put his hands on his hips.

"I'm sorry," Jeremy yelled back. "From where I'm sitting, I'm doing it just like you showed me."

Shep shook his head and swung himself up behind Jeremy on the aging mechanical bull. He lifted Jeremy's arm and stretched it back to the precise position he'd been trying to explain for fifteen minutes. "See? You feel the difference?"

He suddenly noticed that Jeremy had gone stock still in his arms. *Shit.* Maybe he should've thought this through first. The only thing he had going for him was he wasn't sporting an erection. With Jeremy's ass butted against the ridge of his jeans, there would've been no hiding his attraction to the younger man.

Shep released Jeremy's arm and started to dismount. Before he could slide off the back, Jeremy ran his back-stretched hand through Shep's hair. Just that fast, Shep's cock hardened. He quickly shot off the back of the bull and turned his back.

Neither of them spoke for several moments. Finally, Shep found his voice. "Did you feel the difference in that position?"

Jeremy looked him right in the eye and nodded slowly. "Good. That's the money position. You get that right and you're score is guaranteed to go up."

Walking back over to the controls, Shep put his hand on the joystick. "Ready to try it again?"

At the tip of Jeremy's head, Shep started putting the mechanical bull through its paces. "Get that leg kicked out there," he continued to coach. The longer he watched Jeremy's slim hips thrust back and forth, the harder he became until he knew he either needed to excuse himself or come in his jeans.

He quickly shut the bull down and headed towards the door of the barn. "That's all for now. Take a shower and get some sleep."

He couldn't get back to the house fast enough, actually running the last fifty yards.

By the time he shut the front door, he barely had time to unzip his jeans and get his hand around his cock before his seed pumped in rivulets all over his hand and T-shirt.

He was still leaning against the door panting, when the door shook with the force of someone's fist. "Shep, open this door," Jeremy yelled.

Closing his eyes, Shep looked down at the mess he'd made. "Just a minute," he called. The last thing he wanted was for Jeremy to come busting in on him. He quickly walked to the kitchen and washed his hands. Using a wet paper towel, he wiped his cock clean.

He was on his way back to the front door when he remembered the fresh cum on his shirt. "Shit." Shep pulled the shirt over his head and tossed it into the dining room. By the time he reached the door, he was slightly out of breath.

Jeremy pounded again just as Shep opened the door. "What the hell was that all about?" Jeremy asked. He pushed his way past Shep and into the house.

"We were done," Shep answered.

Jeremy stepped forward until he was nose to nose with Shep. "No. We weren't anywhere close to being done." The younger man grabbed the back of Shep's head and kissed him.

Shep's arms automatically wrapped around Jeremy as the kiss went feral, both of them biting and thrusting their tongues into the other's mouth. Shep ran his hands down Jeremy's lean back, to squeeze his ass. Needing to be even closer, he flattened Jeremy against the door and ground his renewed erection against the other man.

"Want you," Jeremy moaned, trying to unfasten Shep's jeans.

Shep grunted his reply, attacking Jeremy's Wranglers. The ringing phone snapped Shep out of his lustful haze. He pulled back and looked into Jeremy's eyes. So young. "We can't do this," he said.

Jeremy looked as though he'd been struck. "What? No," Jeremy said, shaking his head. "After all this time we're finally getting it right. Don't back away from me now."

The phone continued to ring, giving Shep a good excuse to pull away and walk out of the room. "Hello?"

"It's about time you answered. I'd almost given up."

"Hey, Todd." Shep watched Jeremy come into the living room and take a seat on the sofa. With his arms crossed in front of his chest, Shep couldn't help but notice his lean muscular frame.

"I wanted to call to make sure I was still welcome at the ranch. I'm getting in about three days prior to the rodeo."

"Sure," Shep answered without taking his eyes off Jeremy. "You know you're always welcome here." He couldn't read the look on Jeremy's face, but he definitely didn't have trouble reading his body language, as the young man turned and walked out the front door.

"Great. After that last phone conversation I figured I'd better call and make sure before I just showed up with my bags. Is it okay if I bring a friend?"

Taking the phone over to the window, Shep watched Jeremy as he retreated to the bunkhouse. It wasn't like Jeremy to give up on something so easily. Maybe he'd been right. Maybe the kid was still too young for a serious relationship.

"Shep?"

"Yeah. Whatever." Shep heard a high pitched feminine voice in the background.

"Thanks, buddy. Listen, I gotta go, but I'll see you in a couple of weeks."

"Okay. I'll be looking for ya." Shep hung up and walked to the liquor cabinet. He knew if he didn't get the taste of Jeremy's kiss out of his mouth he'd never get to sleep.

The drunker he became, the madder he got. He was of a mind to go to the bunkhouse, pull Jeremy out of bed and demand an explanation. Part of him knew he wasn't making any sense. He was the one who said they shouldn't go any further. *But*, he argued with his drunken self, Jeremy was the one who tried to convince him it was right. The next thing he knew, the man walked out of his house without so much as a goodbye.

Maybe it was the phone call. Why would it be that? Todd always stayed at the ranch for the rodeo. What would make it any different this time? Something just didn't feel right. He finished his drink and slammed the empty glass on the coffee table. "By god, I'll just go find out."

He tried to pull his boots on and ended up ass over tea kettle on the floor. "Fuck 'em," he slurred and walked out the door in his bare feet.

As always, the front door to the bunkhouse was unlocked. "Jeremy?" he yelled, swaying back and forth. "Jeremy! Get your ass out here," he bellowed.

Rance's was the first face he saw pop out of the darkened hallway. "What the hell is going on?"

"Go back to bed. I've got a problem with Jeremy not you."

"I'm here," Jeremy said, wiping the sleep from his eyes.

Shep nearly dropped to his knees at the site of Jeremy in his tight black boxer-briefs. "I wasn't finished talking to you when you stormed out."

By now, Shep noticed several other faces in the hall shadows. He was just sober enough to know he didn't want to discuss his personal life in front of his men. He gestured to the house. "Do you want to come back and talk this out like men, or would you rather have it out right here?"

Jeremy looked over his shoulder at Bo. "What're you lookin' at him for? Can't you make up your own damn mind?" Shep snapped out.

Bo looked at Shep before giving Jeremy a slight nod. "I saw that," Shep bellowed again.

"Come on," Jeremy said and walked out the door without waiting for Shep to follow.

He would of course. He'd follow Jeremy anywhere at this point, but first he needed to know what the hell was going on.

Chapter Five

By the time he stepped into the living room, Jeremy was shaking. He saw the half-empty bottle of whisky on the coffee table and reached for it. Jeremy only managed two big swallows before his hero stumbled into the room.

Shep took the bottle from Jeremy's hand and set it back down. "Why'd you leave like that?"

He didn't know what to say. How could he confess the truth, that his father coming to stay on the ranch scared the shit out of him? "If Dad stays here, I won't be able to enter the rodeo," he finally said, giving Shep only half the truth.

After several blinks and a quick head shake, Shep focused on him once more. "That's it? That's why you walked out without even saying goodbye? Todd always stays here for the rodeo. What made you think this year would be different?" Shep stopped suddenly. "You don't want him to know about us," he seemed to conclude.

No. He didn't want his dad to know, but not for the reasons Shep was conjuring up in his mind. Jeremy knew that if he were to begin a relationship with Shep, he wouldn't be able to keep his secrets. By telling his lover the truth, it would probably end any friendship between Shep and Todd.

Shep took several steps back and fell into one of the brown leather club chairs. "I knew you were too young to know what you wanted. I'm just next in line for you." Shep buried his face in his hands. "I tried to wait. I wanted you to get every other man out of your system before committing to me."

Jeremy's anger with the way Shep had roused him out of bed, fled in a heartbeat. He walked over and knelt in front of the man he'd wanted since the first day they'd met. "No. There isn't anyone else besides you." He wrapped his arms around Shep's calves and rested his cheek against the scarred knee.

The first touch of Shep's hand upon his head, gave him hope. "I don't want my dad here, because I don't like him. I know when he comes it'll be easier to pretend we're not together," Jeremy whispered.

He looked up into Shep's watery blue eyes. "But not for the reason you think."

"Wh…why then?" Shep asked.

"He doesn't approve of me." Jeremy spread his arms wide. "Of anything about me. I've learned to live with it, but you haven't. I want to beat him at the rodeo more than I can ever explain. And if he knows you're helping me train, he'll never forgive you." Jeremy held his breath. He needed Shep to accept as much as he'd dared to tell him.

Shep cupped Jeremy's face in his large rough hands. "Just until after the rodeo?" Shep asked.

"Yeah. After I have a chance to compete against him he'll probably never talk to me again anyway. Give me a little time to say goodbye to him in my own way."

"And until then?"

Jeremy could see the silent plea in Shep's face. He broke away long enough to stand. Arms outstretched, he presented his nearly nude body to his soon-to-be lover. "I'm all yours."

Shep started to grab for him, but Jeremy stopped him with a hand on his chest. "I've always *been* yours, and I'll always *be* yours. We'll just have to be a little more discreet when my dad comes."

He slid his fingers through the short mat of curly hair to brush across Shep's pebbled nipple. "But Dad isn't here yet," Jeremy said, his voice going husky with need.

Shep was on him before he ever finished his sentence, burying his face in Jeremy's brief covered groin. The playful nip to the shaft of his cock, drove all thoughts of his father from his mind. He moved his hands to the back of Shep's head and thrust his hips, seeking more.

His cock was mouthed and licked until his briefs were sodden. "Please," he choked out.

Shep grasped the elastic waistband and drew the tight boxers over Jeremy's hips and down his legs. As his cock was engulfed by Shep's warm mouth, Jeremy kicked out of his underwear and put a foot on the chair beside his lover's hip.

He watched as Shep's tongue dipped into the slit at the tip of his cock. His man was rewarded with a large drop of pre-cum. "Mmm," Shep moaned.

"Suck it," Jeremy groaned, pressing harder against the back of Shep's head.

"Gladly," Shep answered.

Jeremy watched as his cock was devoured. The sight of Shep's lips stretched thin as they surrounded his girth had been a fantasy for years. Jeremy couldn't count the number of times he'd jerked off with this picture in mind. How many nameless cowboys had he been with that he'd closed his eyes and pretended were Shep? All of them. He'd never once had sex without wishing it was with the man now sucking his cock.

Feeling his balls draw up, Jeremy grabbed a handful of Shep's hair. "I can't hold it," he warned.

Shep's answer was to slide Jeremy's dick even further down his throat. When his lover lightly clenched his teeth around the thick base of Jeremy's cock, he lost it, shooting his seed.

Shep pulled off enough to swallow every drop as Jeremy's body vibrated with the force of his release. "Never," he gasped. "So good."

After licking him clean, Shep sat back in his chair and rubbed his hand over the wet spot of his crotch. "Need you," Shep growled.

Jeremy unfastened Shep's jeans and pulled them off, tossing them to the side. He started to kneel, but his lover stopped him. "No. I need *you*."

He looked around the room. "Stuff?"

"Dammit," Shep cursed. "Upstairs."

Jeremy wasted no time pulling the still tipsy man out of his chair. "Let's go."

* * * *

After digging around in his bathroom vanity for what seemed like hours, Shep finally found a condom. He almost gave up and went back downstairs, knowing both he and Jeremy had one in their wallet. "Yes," he crowed, as his fingers closed around the square foil packet.

Stepping back into the bedroom, he stopped. Jeremy's skin seemed to glow in the soft light of his bedside lamp. His young lover had already found the bottle of lube and was stretching his own ass.

Without breaking eye contact, Jeremy added a third slim digit and moaned. "Fuck," Shep said in a reverent tone. He felt his balls begin to draw up and quickly squeezed the soft skin where they met his body, pulling them back down. *Not yet. Please, just let me get inside of him first.* He used his teeth to rip open the wrapper and quickly sheathed his dripping cock.

"Sexy fucker," he said, knocking Jeremy's hand away from what was his. After dribbling another thin stream of lube down the crack of Jeremy's ass, he fit his cockhead to the stretched opening and slowly pushed his way inside.

Jeremy's sharp hiss stopped him. "Am I hurting you?" Shep managed to ask.

His lover shook his head from side to side against the pillow. "More," Jeremy begged.

With one deep thrust, Shep's cock was buried to the root. He felt his balls slap against Jeremy's ass with the force of his drive. Shep stopped and tried to get himself under control once more. "I've waited years for this moment."

"I wish I'd known," Jeremy panted, as Shep pulled out and surged back in.

He set a fast, penetrating rhythm in and out of Jeremy's sweet ass. Rarely had he found a partner who could take all of him their first time together. It only proved to Shep that Jeremy was meant to be his.

Needing to be even deeper, Shep lifted his lover's hips off the bed without breaking his stride.

"Harder," Jeremy cried.

Fuck. He pulled out and slapped Jeremy's ass. "Hands and knees."

His lover quickly rolled and presented his well-stretched hole once more. "I don't break," Jeremy said, looking over his shoulder.

In one thrust, Shep was once again buried to the hilt. He placed both hands on Jeremy's shoulder for leverage as he pounded his lover with all his strength and passion.

With his hands braced against the headboard, Jeremy continued to call out Shep's name as he rocked back into the forceful thrusts. With a quick change of angles, Shep pegged Jeremy's pleasure gland over and over.

The clenching of Jeremy's body as he spilt his seed onto the comforter below was a welcomed gift to Shep. He'd held on as long as he could, waiting for his lover to come first. With a roar, Shep came. His cock pulsing with stream after stream of cum.

Afraid he'd filled the condom to capacity, he quickly pulled out before he had a chance to soften. He knew he was clean, but he wouldn't chance Jeremy's safety for anything. As he fell to the bed beside his lover, he pinched the condom around his cock. It wasn't until he regained the control of his breathing that he slipped the used rubber off and tied it into a knot. Dropping it over the side of the bed, he was pleased when he heard the ting as it landed in the metal trashcan.

Shep reached over and turned off the light, before wrapping himself around Jeremy. He still couldn't believe what had just happened. His love for the younger man was so strong that he wanted to shout it from the rooftop, but he stopped himself. Jeremy deserved to process all that had happened before hearing declarations of love from a washed up bull rider.

His lover was so quiet Shep thought he'd drifted off to sleep. He kissed the back of Jeremy's neck as he settled his head on the pillow.

"You said you'd waited years. What did you mean?" Jeremy whispered in the now dark room.

Shep's whole body stiffened. Did he dare tell him the truth? Would Jeremy think he was a pervert?

"Shep?" Jeremy prompted.

"The first time I saw you wrapped in nothing but a towel, I knew." Shep put some distance between them in case he needed to shield a blow. "I think you were about seventeen. Hell, maybe sixteen. I'm not proud of myself. I think it's the reason..."

"Shhh," Jeremy said, cutting him off. His lover turned over and pressed a kiss against Shep's lips. "It's what I wanted. I paraded my half-nude body around you as much as I could get away with. I wanted you from the first moment I laid eyes on you. It's the reason I came out to dad the night he took me home to the trailer the two of you shared."

Jeremy kissed him again. "I wanted you to know I'd welcome any advance on your part."

Shep shook his head. "You were too young. Hell, you're still too young." Shep ran his hand over Jeremy's closely cropped hair. "I had to fuck a lot of cowboys before I was ready to settle down with just one. I wanted...no, I needed you to get other men out of your system first."

Jeremy surprised him by flipping one long leg over his stomach and straddling him. Looking down, Jeremy shook his head. "The only reason I ever let another cowboy fuck me was so I'd be ready for you when the time came. I've never wanted or needed anyone else. I'd heard stories about all the men you'd fucked and didn't want to disappoint you."

Shep pulled his lover down against his chest. "I would've taught you myself had I known."

There didn't seem to be anything else left to say at the moment. Shep rubbed loving circles into Jeremy's back as the younger man's breathing slowed. The soft snore coming from Jeremy made him smile. He knew he could happily sleep in this position for the rest of his days.

They still had the matter with Todd to work out, but he had no doubt he'd gladly give up his best friend for the man in his arms.

Chapter Six

Shep was bent over his keyboard when Jeremy came bouncing into the office. "You feel like going with me to pre-register later?" Jeremy asked.

Tossing his glasses onto the desk, Shep stood and pulled his lover into his arms. "Only if you agree to have dinner with me afterwards."

"Hmmm," Jeremy pretended to think about the offer. "I guess I could do that. Although I was really looking forward to Frank's sloppy joe sandwiches."

Shep reached down and pinched Jeremy's ass. "I'll make it worth your while." They'd spent every night for a week in each other's arms and he'd never felt happier.

Jeremy grinned and rubbed his jean covered cock across Shep's zipper. "You always do."

"Shep!" Rance called, running into the office. His foreman skidded to a stop, eyes as big as saucers. "Sorry to interrupt, but something's wrong with Dynamo."

Shep was heading towards the front door before Rance had a chance to continue. "Buddy found him on his side out in the pasture. He said he tried, but the damn fool won't get up and his breathing is laboured. I put a call into Jeb Garza. He's out at the EZ doctoring a heifer, but said he'd be here shortly," Rance explained as the three of them hopped into the pickup.

Rance jumped out and unlocked the pasture gate. "How late is registration open?" Shep asked, giving Jeremy's thigh a squeeze.

"Doesn't matter," Jeremy answered as Shep drove into the pasture and waited for his foreman to relock the gate.

Before Rance had a chance to get back in, Shep leaned over and placed a soft kiss on Jeremy's lips. "It does matter. I'll get you there one way or another."

Rance hopped in and pointed in the direction of the downed bull. Shep took off across the pasture. By the time he spotted Buddy standing beside the bull, he was sure his brains were permanently rattled.

Shep pulled to a stop. Before he'd even made it to Dynamo's side, Buddy held his hands up and walked towards him. "Sorry, Boss."

Ignoring Buddy's outstretched hands, Shep continued on to one of his favourite bulls. It was evident the old man was dead. He turned back to Buddy. "What happened?"

Buddy shook his head and put his hands on his hips. "Convulsions started about twenty minutes ago. He passed just before you drove up."

Shep stripped his hat off and threw it on the ground. Looking out over the pasture, he let out a string of

Carol Lynne

curses. "It's obvious he ate something." He took off across the pasture towards the slow running stream, scanning the grass as he went. He noticed the other three men spread out and follow his lead.

With a sinking feeling, he neared the creek. What he saw spurned another round of cussing. "Who the fuck's job was it to spray the pasture this year?" he asked Rance.

Rance stepped up beside Shep and looked at the toxic cowbane plant at the edge of the water. "Fuck," Rance spat out. "It was Contrell's job. Shit. I should've known to go behind him and check his work." Rance looked at Shep. "I take full responsibility, Boss."

"You shouldn't have to double check your men's work. I'm almost sorry we already fired that sonofabitch. Do you know if he's still in the county?"

Rance shook his head. "Last I heard he was headed to Montana to work on a ranch there."

"Get me the name and phone number of the ranch owner. He deserves to know what kind of slack-assed man he has working for him."

"Yes, Boss."

"And get Bo and every other man you can spare out in the pastures. I want every square inch of grazing land gone over and spot treated before another one of my animals is released out here."

Bo nodded and took off across the pasture with Buddy in tow. Shep started walking back to Dynamo. They'd have to get Jeb out here to write up the paperwork for the insurance company before they could bury the poor bull.

He could hear the swishing of the grass as Jeremy walked behind him. Stopping, he waited for his man to catch up and held out his hand.

"I'm sorry," Jeremy said, taking Shep's offered hand. "I know he was one of your best."

"Such a waste. I should've never hired that lazy fucker." He walked them over to the shade and wrapped his arms around Jeremy.

Jeremy nipped Shep's jaw. "Wanna neck until Doc Garza gets here?" Jeremy asked playfully.

Shep grinned. Just that fast, Jeremy had him feeling better. "I don't know if that would be such a good idea. You know we have a tendency to get carried away, and I'll be damned if I want Jeb getting a look of that pretty ass of yours."

Jeremy ground against Shep's fly. "Your ass."

"Mine," Shep said giving the fine ass in question a good squeeze.

* * * *

Jeremy checked the sky. It had to be going on close to six o'clock. He wondered for the hundredth time whether Carol would still be at the city hall by the time they got there. They had pretty much shut down the entire ranch to check the pastures and now that he'd gone over his last section, he looked around for Shep.

He spotted him a few moments later coming over the rise on the front loader. Shep had insisted on burying Dynamo himself, refusing all offers of help. Jeremy couldn't believe a man who'd once had the shit stomped out of him could still hold a soft spot for the thirteen hundred pound bull.

The tractor rolled to a stop several feet away from him. He waved and climbed up to the air conditioned cab. "You done?" Shep asked.

"Yep, just a few minutes ago. You?"

"Yeah. Let me get the tractor back in the barn and wash up real quick and we can go."

Jeremy leaned in and gave Shep a quick kiss. "I'll drive the truck back, and meet you in the shower."

Shep chuckled. "You do that and we'll never make it to town in time."

"Shoot. You're right. I'll take one in the bunkhouse and meet you in thirty minutes." After another quick kiss he hopped down from the tractor and jogged to the truck. "Anyone who's ready, I'm going back!" he yelled.

Bo swung into the passenger seat, as four guys climbed in the bed. "You find anything?" Bo asked as they headed towards home.

"Nope, but better safe than sorry," Jeremy answered. "You?"

"A small pocket of milkweed over on the west side of the pasture." Bo shook his head. "If I were Shep I'd be pissed."

"Oh he was, believe me," Jeremy chuckled. He stopped and waited for Bo to open the gate before driving through. "I'm going to take a quick shower and then head to town. Do you need anything?"

"Nope, can't think of anything. I'd say a cinnamon roll, but I doubt Kyle is open this time of night. And I'm dirtier than you are, so it's only fair I shower first."

"Shep and I are going so I can pre-register for the rodeo and grab a bite to eat. You wouldn't want to make me late would ya?" He parked the truck on the other side of the barn and got out. Looking over at Bo he winked. "Race you to the showers."

"You're on," Bo said, as they both took off running.

Laughing, Jeremy passed Bo when the older man had to stop to open the door. "Cheater," Bo yelled when he caught up to Jeremy in the bathroom. "At least there's more than one."

They both stripped and got into their individual stalls, separated by a short, chest-high wall. The cool water felt so good after his hot day in the pasture. He was used to being in the barn or arena more than outside. "I don't know how you do it," he commented.

"Do what?" Bo asked, rinsing the shampoo from his shoulder-length dark brown hair.

"Work in the hayfield all day. It must be boring and hot as hell." He took a whiff of the herbal scented shampoo before pouring a small amount into his palm.

Bo shrugged. "It's not for everyone, but I love it. Gives me time to think."

"What could you possibly have to think about all day, every day?" He rinsed the suds from his hair and looked at Bo.

"I don't know…life and shit. I sent the divorce papers to my wife last week. She says she's cool with it, but there's something in her voice that's been bugging me." Bo turned off his water and reached for a towel on the shelf just outside the shower.

Jeremy followed suit. "Toss me one of those, will ya?"

Bo flung him a towel and walked out of the bathroom without saying anything else. Jeremy watched the bronzed back leave the room. *Was it something I said?* He dried off quickly and wrapped his towel around his hips.

Stepping into the bedroom he shared with Bo, he began to worry. "Bo? Did I say something to piss you off?"

Bo stepped into one of the sarong, skirt-like things that everyone teased him about. "Not really. Just thinking about Jan." Bo shook his head. "I don't like hurting people."

Jeremy hung his towel on the hook on the back of the door and pulled on his underwear. "I thought you said she was cool with it?"

"Yeah. She says she is, but I can't stop worrying that there's something she's not telling me."

"Could she be pregnant?" Jeremy selected a short sleeved snap front shirt from his small closet and put it on.

Bo scowled at him. "I'm HIV positive. Do you think I'd make love to anyone without protection?"

"No," Jeremy said defensively. "I'm trying to cheer you up and all I'm managing to do is piss you off even more. I'm sorry."

Bo walked over and gave Jeremy a hug. "Don't be sorry," Bo said, continuing the hug. "Truth be told, I thought of the same thing. I don't think that's it, though."

"What the hell is going on?"

Jeremy's head snapped towards the door and an angry looking lover. "Hey. I'm ready," he said to

Shep. He knew he wasn't doing anything wrong, so he refused to feel guilty for giving comfort to a friend.

He looked into Bo's black eyes. "You gonna be okay?"

"Sure," Bo grinned. "I always land on my feet."

By the time Bo broke away and Jeremy joined Shep, he could feel the anger emanating from the man. "Come on." He walked passed Shep who was still standing like a statue with his arms crossed in front of his chest.

By the time Shep got into the pickup, Jeremy was well on his way to being pissed off. "You want to tell me what that was all about?" Jeremy asked.

"Funny. I was going to ask you the same thing," Shep countered. "Do I have something to be worried about?"

"Dammit," Jeremy spat out. "I was giving comfort to a goddamn friend. Nothing more. Get over yourself."

Those blue eyes stared at him for several moments before Shep sighed. "I'm sorry. I guess I let my imagination get the better of me."

"Nothing but comfort was being given," Jeremy reminded his lover.

"Okay, yeah, you said that already. But how would you feel if you walked into my bedroom and saw me and Rance in an embrace?"

Jeremy pictured the two men together. Yeah. It would definitely get under his skin. As a matter of fact, he'd probably go nuts. "I see what you're saying. Just don't use that analogy around Bo. I might not be big enough to take the both of you on, but Bo wouldn't give it a second thought."

Shep pulled Jeremy into his arms and kissed him. "You telling me that Bo has a crush on me?"

Jeremy started laughing. "Hell no. Do you think he'd be my friend if that were the case? No. Bo definitely has eyes for only one man and that's Rance."

Shep started the truck. "He's wasting his time."

They pulled out of the drive and headed towards town. Jeremy moulded himself to Shep's side and kissed his neck. "Why would you say something like that? Bo's a good looking guy. He's funny and sweet…"

"Enough," Shep elbowed him in the side. "It's not Bo. It's Rance. He was the first man I hired when I built the place, and I've never known him to take a lover in all that time."

"Hmmm." He knew there had to be a story there, but decided to drop the whole thing.

"I talked to Carol, by the way. She said she'd stick around until we got there. Luckily, she has a sweet spot for me."

Jeremy laughed. "Liar. That woman doesn't have a sweet spot for anyone."

Shep grinned. "Okay. I told her I'd give her fifty bucks if she stayed."

"Now that sounds more like Carol."

Chapter Seven

Shep couldn't help notice the way Jeremy's hand shook as he filled out the registration form. When they left city hall, he pointed towards Booklovers. "Mind if we stop before we eat? Naomi's holding a new book on insemination for me."

Jeremy chuckled and shook his head. "As long as it's about inseminating four legged creatures and not two legged."

He laughed and pulled Jeremy closer to his side. "Not unless you plan to make medical history." Shep opened the door and stepped inside the cool interior. He wished he had more time for pleasure reading. There was just something magical about a bookstore.

"Hey, guys," Naomi said.

"Hey, Naomi," Shep greeted. "Thought I'd come in and pick up my book you've been holding."

"Okey dokey, coming right up." Naomi bounced off towards the back of the store.

"She's cute, isn't she?" Shep mused. There was just something about the red headed sprite that made him smile.

Jeremy smacked the back of his head. "Wipe the smile off your face before I get jealous."

Coming back into the room, Naomi held her arms in the air, the book in one hand. "Don't shoot. I promise you have nothing to worry about from me."

Shep chuckled as Jeremy turned red.

"You weren't supposed to hear that," Jeremy mumbled.

"Oh, but I hear everything," Naomi said in a stage whisper. She handed the book to Shep. "Is there anything else I can get ya?"

"Nope, this is it." They walked to the sales counter. "So what are you doing here this late in the evening? Where's Melissa?"

Naomi rolled her eyes. "That'll be twenty-seven fifty. Melissa's in Sheridan taking a night class. I don't mind really. It's not like I have anything better to do. I might as well spend my time waiting on two handsome cowboys."

"You're good for my ego," Shep chuckled, taking his change.

Naomi covered his hand where it rested on the counter. "It's good to see you so happy."

He looked at Jeremy. "It's good to feel this happy. You'll find it when you least expect it."

"From your lips to God's ears," Naomi said.

They left Booklovers and stood on the sidewalk. "What do you think? Canoe?"

"Wow. Going all out. Is this our first official date?" Jeremy asked as he batted his long black lashes.

It suddenly occurred to him that he hadn't taken Jeremy anywhere. He could blame it on the fact that he'd never really dated, but the truth was, by the end of the day, he just wanted Jeremy to himself. "Yeah. I'm sorry, I guess it is our first official date. Remind me to take you out more. I'm not really used to it."

"I was teasing," Jeremy said. They walked across and down the street to Canoe. "In case you haven't noticed, I'm a pretty low maintenance kind of guy. I like quiet nights at home just as much as you do."

"Good, because even though I don't mind going out occasionally, I'd much rather be home snuggled up with you." Shep opened the heavy restaurant door and held it for Jeremy. He slipped a proprietary hand on Jeremy's lower back in case Erico was around. He used to think it was funny when the restaurant owner and chef flirted with the customers, but that was before he had someone to lose. "Stick close," he said in Jeremy's ear.

Shep needn't have worried. He quickly discovered that Erico was in San Francisco trying to hire some sous-chef he'd heard about. Shep wished the guy luck. Erico went through chefs like no one's business.

On the drive home, he spread his thighs as Jeremy's hand began to wander. "Keep this up and we won't make it into the house." He wasn't about to tell his lover to stop, especially when Jeremy began unfastening his jeans. It had been a hell of a long time since he'd had a hand job while behind the wheel.

Shep moaned as Jeremy lay down in the seat and licked a path up his engorged cock. It had been even longer since he'd been given a blowjob while driving. He took one hand off the wheel and ran it down

Jeremy's back. He tried to slip between his lover's skin and the waistband of his jeans with no luck. "As much as I love these painted on Wranglers, I'd much prefer to feel your ass right about now."

Without taking his mouth off Shep's cock, Jeremy reached under him and unfastened his jeans, pushing them down his thighs. Shep groaned as his cowboy scooted up on his knees, presenting his ass to perfection. "Damn you're sexy."

Jeremy wiggled his ass until Shep licked a finger and entered his lover's puckered hole. A deep guttural moan from Jeremy sent vibrations down the length of Shep's cock straight to his balls.

He took his foot off the accelerator and let the truck coast to a crawl as he thrust up into his man's willing mouth. "Ready? I can't hold it anymore."

Jeremy's nod was all the permission he needed before spilling the contents of his balls. Even as his seed shot down Jeremy's throat, Shep continued the plunging assault on his lover's ass, until he heard the cowboy's cries of completion.

Shep pulled Jeremy into his arms and kissed him, tasting his own cum. "Damn," he said with a grin.

Jeremy licked Shep's jaw and down his neck. "Get us home. Now that my ass is stretched, I want a good long ride before bed."

They set their clothes to rights, and Shep put his foot back on the gas. After the day they'd had, Shep wanted nothing more than to lose himself inside of his lover.

The black dual-cab pickup parked in front of the house, shocked them both. "Fuck," Jeremy cursed. "What's he doing here so early?"

Shep shook his head. He wondered how Todd's early arrival would affect his relationship with Jeremy for the next week and a half. His answer came sooner than he thought.

"Drop me off at the bunkhouse," Jeremy said.

Shep wrapped his arm tighter around his lover. "Are you sure this is what you want? To be hidden away like some secret lover?"

Jeremy nodded and kissed Shep's cheek. "It's the only way. If Dad's focus isn't on me, then he won't know I'm planning to compete in the rodeo."

Shep pulled to a stop in front of the bunkhouse. He started to say he didn't want to be parted from his love for the next ten days, but a kiss from Jeremy stopped him. "Please," Jeremy begged. "I have to compete. As much as I love you, I have to do this."

"Okay," he agreed. He gave Jeremy one last kiss and watched his lover walk away. As he drove back to the house, the hair on the back of his neck stood. It was the same feeling he'd had when Jeremy had first asked for his help in training. Why was it so important for his lover to keep the information from his own father?

His thoughts were cut short by the opening of his front door. Todd and a tiny blonde stood in the brightly lit doorway. Turning off the truck, Shep got out and climbed the steps. "You're early," he said, embracing his friend. He acknowledged to himself that Todd was no longer his best friend. That position had clearly been taken by the man's son, and Shep wouldn't have had it any other way.

Todd shrugged. "I decided not to compete in this weekend's events. Thought maybe it would be better to visit my old friend and prepare for next weekend's competition instead."

As Shep led the way to the living room, he rubbed the back of his neck. It struck him as odd that Todd hadn't mentioned the need to see his son.

He went immediately to the bar and fixed Todd his usual scotch and water. Turning, he held the drink out to his friend. "And what can I get you?" he asked Todd's buckle bunny.

"Sorry, I've forgotten my manners," Todd said. "This is Regina. She'll have a gin and tonic if you have it?"

Shep nodded and found what he needed. Twisting the cap off a new bottle of tonic, he studied his old friend. Something was definitely different, but he couldn't put his finger on what, something in Todd's eyes.

"So," Todd began. "How's business?"

Gesturing to the couch, Shep handed Regina her drink and opened a bottle of water for himself. "I lost Dynamo to cowbane. Buried the ornery sonofabitch a few hours ago."

"Damn," Todd said. "He was one of your biggest money-makers, too."

Shep nodded. It wasn't the money he'd miss as much as the thrill of watching Dynamo perform for the crowds. "Other than that, everything's good. The breeding program is taking off and we have quite a few good bulls coming of age."

He hated to admit he hadn't kept up on his friend's career. "How's the season been? Any new hotshots?"

Todd got a funny look on his face, before quickly covering it with his drink. "You know how it is, there's always some young rider nipping at your heels."

"I imagine so." He looked from Todd to Regina, who was curled against the champion's side. "Would you like another?" he pointed towards Regina's glass once he noticed it was empty. Damn, the woman could drink.

"Please," she giggled.

After fixing both of his guests another glass, he glanced at the clock. "I hope you don't think I'm being rude, but it's been a hell of a long day. Would it be okay if we talked more at breakfast?"

"You go on to bed," Todd said, blatantly squeezing Regina's triple D breast. "I'm sure we'll find something to occupy us. Right, baby?"

Regina just giggled. Shep wondered, not for the first time, if the size of the woman's chest was the only thing Todd saw in her.

"You know where the guest room is," Shep said as he tossed his empty water bottle into the trashcan. "Goodnight."

"Night," Todd moaned as Regina's long fingernails scraped across the fly of his jeans.

Shep rolled his eyes and walked out of the room. He looked at the front door as he passed, wanting nothing more than to go to his lover.

With a sigh of resignation, Shep walked up the stairs to his own bed. Now that he was used to Jeremy sleeping practically on top of him, Shep knew it would be a long night.

* * * *

Jeremy settled into bed shortly after Shep dropped him off. He hated keeping things from his lover, but saw no other way. If Shep knew what Todd had done to him…

"Something wrong? You and Shep still fighting over that hug I gave you earlier?" Bo asked from the bed beside him.

"No. My dad's here. His truck was in front of the house when we pulled up."

"And you don't want him to know you and Shep are together," Bo surmised on his own.

"Right. I need to keep him in the dark until the competition. I need to compete against him, and I can't very well do that if Shep kills him first."

"You're taking a big chance. Shep's gonna be pissed when he finds out what you've been keeping from him. You know that, right?"

He hadn't really thought of it. Now that he did, he was suddenly afraid Bo was right. Would Shep feel betrayed? Or god forbid, used?

"Shit. One more thing to worry about," he said, exasperated.

"Only you can decide which is more important." He heard Bo's sheets rustle as his friend shifted on his bed. "Good night."

"Night." Jeremy had a lot to think about. He only hoped ten days would be enough time.

Chapter Eight

For two days, Shep watched Todd and Jeremy skirt each other. The only time he saw his lover was either in the arena during their secret training sessions, or in the barn. Never once did Jeremy come to the house to seek out his father, and likewise, Todd never asked about his son. Something was definitely going on between the two men.

He found Todd in the kitchen on the morning of the third day. "I invited Jeremy for dinner," he announced.

Todd looked momentarily shocked, but quickly hid his expression. "You invite all your hired hands to dinner?"

Shep's chest constricted at the cold words of his friend. "No, but Jeremy's more than a hired hand. I noticed you hadn't spent any time together, so I thought this would be a good way for the two of you to catch up."

Todd shrugged. "We don't see eye to eye on most things. He changed a lot after you retired."

Once again, Shep wondered if Todd resented the fact that his only son was gay. He decided to stop beating around the bush. "Because he's gay? I thought you didn't have a problem with homosexuals."

Todd laughed. "I don't have a problem with fags in general, as long as they keep it behind closed doors. It's a son who feels the need to crow his preferences to the world that I admit to having a problem with."

Did that mean Jeremy was openly promiscuous when he lived with Todd? And what the hell was the deal with using the word fags? He'd had more than one discussion with his friend over that particular term. Todd's next statement cleared up a few things in Shep's mind.

"He's the reason some of my sponsors have been cutting me loose. No one wants the father of a fag hocking boots and sports drinks."

Shep's eyes narrowed as he leaned over the table to get in Todd's face. "If you use that term one more time in my home, I'll kick your ass."

Todd held his hands up in mock-surrender. "Take it easy. I've no desire to fight with you. You asked a question and I'm just explaining. Geeze."

"Well, explain without the colourful metaphors, will ya?" Shep sat back down just as Regina sauntered into the room.

"Morning," she said. Shep watched the woman out of the corner of his eye as she filled a cup with coffee and joined them at the table. "Sugar, will you take me into town? I want to find something special to wear to the street dance." She bounced in her chair. "Oh, did you hear that Trick Allen is going to perform? He's soooo dreamy."

Todd gave a nervous chuckle. He openly caressed Regina's breast and narrowed his eyes. "Don't you go getting ideas about Trick Allen. I'd hate to have to crush the man's vocal chords."

Unable to stomach any more of the blatant sex play, Shep rose. "I'd better get busy. You all have a nice afternoon of shopping."

As he headed towards the barn, he wondered if Todd had always been such an ass, or if the changes were new.

* * * *

Opening the front door, Shep knew he had a precious few minutes to greet his lover before Todd and Regina strolled down the stairs. He pulled Jeremy into his arms and devoured his mouth. "Miss you. Miss this," he said, before kissing him again.

"Meet me in the barn later," Jeremy whispered.

His lover pulled away when they heard the tread of feet at the top of the stairs. "Count on it," he whispered back.

"Dinner's ready," Shep said as Todd and Regina made it to the bottom of the steps.

"Dad," Jeremy said with a nod. His lover looked Regina up and down. "You're new," he commented.

"I'd like you to meet Regina. Baby, this is my son, Jeremy."

Shep was proud of his lover as he held out his hand in greeting. Regina looked up at Todd for several heart beats before hesitantly acknowledging Jeremy's offered greeting. "Your father has told me about you," she said, quickly dropping her hand from Jeremy's.

"I bet he hasn't told you everything," Jeremy added, staring straight into his father's eyes.

Shep could feel the hostility in the air. He concluded that the two men honestly no longer liked each other. "Dinner?" he prompted and gestured towards the dining room.

He pressed a comforting hand against the small of Jeremy's back as his guests preceded him. Although he knew Jeremy didn't want to draw attention to his skills, Shep couldn't help but to boast on his lover. "Jeremy's been a great asset to the ranch."

"Yeah?" Todd seemed to question. "You a good shit shoveler?"

Before Jeremy could say anything, Shep came to his defence. "Rance has him putting the bulls through their paces. He's damn good at his job, too."

The look of open hostility on Todd's face shocked him. Jeremy's head whipped towards Shep. "I'm okay," Jeremy mumbled.

Shep decided to keep his mouth shut until he could question his lover. Something was definitely being kept from him and he planned to find out exactly what it was. First though, they had to get through dinner.

* * * *

Shep excused himself shortly after Jeremy's exit, using the excuse that he needed to check on something in the barn. The rest of dinner had been torturous with the glares between father and son, and Regina's incessant giggling.

By the time he found his lover, he was almost livid. "What the hell is going on?" he asked.

Jeremy quickly hopped off the mechanical bull and stood in front of him. "What do you mean?"

"Don't play dumb. It doesn't suit you. What the hell is going on between you and Todd? And don't give me any shit. I want the truth."

He watched as Jeremy's mouth opened and closed, his Adam's apple bobbing. "Well?" Shep prompted, when his lover said nothing.

Jeremy turned away and looked towards the dirt floor. "He doesn't want me to ride," Jeremy confessed. "He never has."

Shep's anger began to dissipate at the defeated look of his lover. He took the steps required to put his arms around Jeremy's waist. "Oh, love, he just worries about you. That's what father's do."

Jeremy laughed. The sound so cold it sent a shiver up Shep's spine. "It has nothing to do with me getting hurt. He's afraid I'll beat him."

Shep froze. He thought back over everything that had happened. Todd sending Jeremy to live at the ranch was just the start. Did Todd really want his son out of the way? Knowing his friend's competitive streak and desire to always be on top, he didn't doubt his lover's words.

Jeremy turned in his arms and buried his face in Shep's hair. "I didn't want you to know. At first I was afraid that you'd honour his wishes and refuse to let me ride. Then I was in your bed, and I worried what you'd do if you found out." Jeremy planted kisses on

Shep's neck and jaw. "I don't want to lose you, not because of him. I know he's your best friend and I…"

"Shhh," Shep soothed. He tilted Jeremy's head up to look him in the eyes. "I love you. *You're* my best friend."

Jeremy's eyes glistened with unshed tears. "I love you, too. More than any damn rodeo. I'll drop out."

"No," Shep barked. "You need to do this."

"Not if I run the risk of losing you," Jeremy said.

Shep gave Jeremy's shoulder a gentle shake. "You're not going to lose me. Hell, I've waited my entire life for a man like you. I'll be damned if I'll let Todd's insecurities get in the way of that."

He brushed his thumb over the healing cut on Jeremy's lean face. "I've never had to worry about anyone else's safety on the back of a bull. You'll have to be patient with me," he grinned.

Jeremy leaned into Shep's touch. "Whatever happens to me, I need to do this. It's time I finally stood up for myself and walked out of the shadow cast by my father."

Shep understood what Jeremy was saying. It didn't mean that he still didn't worry. "And what happens when you step out of Todd's shadow? What if you win? Will you leave Cattle Valley for the fame and fortune of the PBR?" he asked, voicing his greatest concern.

Jeremy shook his head. "I've had my fill of living on the road. There's no place I'd rather be than here in your bed every night for the rest of my life."

Shep crushed his mouth to Jeremy's, putting all the love he felt into a series of kisses. For the third night in a row, Shep knew he'd get very little sleep, but this time, for a completely different reason.

* * * *

Jeremy woke with Shep's solid body pressed to his back. The unmistakable length of his lover's morning erection was pushed against his ass in the narrow bed. He opened his eyes and was more than a little surprised to see Bo staring straight at them. "Good morning," Jeremy whispered.

"I can see that," Bo said with a smile. "It's going on six. Unless something changed overnight, you might want to wake the boss and have him head out before his guests wake up."

Jeremy nodded. "Can you give us a few minutes?"

"Sure." Bo threw back the covers and swung his legs over the side of the bed. Before he left the room, Bo turned back. "Did you tell him everything?"

"Almost," he whispered.

Bo looked at him for several seconds before retreating from the bedroom. "What haven't you told me?" Shep's deep voice asked in his ear.

Shit. He'd worried about this moment since the first time his dad had struck him. He knew, even before they became lovers, what Shep's reaction would be. "If I tell you, you'll send Dad away, and then I won't get the chance to compete against him."

Shep scooted back enough to turn Jeremy in his arms. Nose to nose, Shep looked into Jeremy's eyes.

He didn't dare say anything, and for several long moments, neither did Shep. Suddenly, it was like a light went on in Shep's head. His lover ran his finger across Jeremy's cheek. "Did he do this?"

Jeremy swallowed. "When I went to see him, he pissed me off. So, I told him I was going to ride in the rodeo and this time I'd get to finish, then we'd see who the better man was. I know it was stupid, but I..."

"I'll kill him." Shep jumped out of bed and reached for his jeans.

"No, please. This is why I didn't want you to know. Please, Shep," Jeremy begged, wrapping his arms around his lover's bare torso.

Shep stopped dressing and cupped Jeremy's face. "Even if I didn't love you as much as I do, I'd never be able to stand back knowing that monster laid a hand on you."

"Please, not yet," Jeremy continued to beg.

"The only thing I can promise is that I'll make sure he still competes."

"How?" Jeremy asked.

"Leave that to me," Shep said and kissed him. "I'll come find you after I take out the trash."

Jeremy watched as Shep's broad muscled back left his room, shirt in hand. He quickly dressed and went to find Rance.

Chapter Nine

Shep took the stairs two at a time, busting into Todd's room without knocking. He walked over and kicked the bed hard enough to wake both Todd and Regina. "Get your bags packed and get the hell out of my house!"

Regina quickly reached for the sheet to cover her exposed nudity. "Wh...what's going on?" she squeaked.

Shep didn't bother to answer the blonde bimbo. He focused on Todd and his dawning awareness of what was going on. "What the hell is wrong with you?" Todd asked, reaching for a pair of jeans.

"How dare you lay a hand on your own son, you bastard."

"What? He told you that? He's lying. He lies all the time."

Shep was on Todd in a flash, wrapping his hands around the man's throat. "I'll kill you," he screamed.

"Shep! Stop," a voice shouted.

Someone was behind him trying to pry his hands off the man in his grip. "Don't do this," Rance said in his ear. "He may be an asshole, but he's still Jeremy's father, and your friend."

Shep looked into Todd's red face. He was fascinated by the way his long-time friend was slowly turning purple.

"Please," a soft voice to the side of him said.

Jeremy's voice was the only thing that had the power to break the spell of rage that had overtaken him. He released Todd and pushed him back on the bed. "Five minutes. You've got five minutes to get out, or I'll finish the job I started."

Always the man of reason, Rance stepped between Shep and Todd. "Let's go downstairs while they pack."

Shep turned and pulled Jeremy into his arms.

"It'll be okay," Jeremy said and led Shep from the room.

By the time Jeremy sat him in a kitchen chair, Shep had begun to shake. He could've very well killed his friend, his ex-friend. Rance handed him a cup of coffee, but his hands were shaking so badly he couldn't even hold the cup.

Jeremy took the coffee from him and set it on the table. He crawled into Shep's lap and held him. "I shouldn't have told you."

The sadness in his lover's voice snapped him out of the trance-like state he was in. "No. Don't say that. I wish you would've told me as soon as it happen..." Shep stopped as something occurred to him. "He's done this before, hasn't he? When was the first time?"

Jeremy looked down, refusing to meet Shep's eyes. "My ribs. Remember I told you that I entered a competition a couple years ago? Well, after my first ride, Dad found me and shoved me into one of the chutes. That's why I couldn't finish."

He still couldn't believe the man he'd called friend for so many years was capable of such a thing. "What happened to him? He sounds like a stranger to me."

"I'll tell you what happened," Todd said, standing in the doorway. "I inherited a fag for a son who thought he was man enough to take me on."

Shep sprang up off his chair, setting Jeremy on his feet. He started to advance, but both Rance and Jeremy were there to stop him. "I warned you about using that word in my house."

"Am I hitting too close to home, Shep? There was a time when you thought you could outride me as well." Todd sneered. "You should've stuck with the Gay Rodeo Association. Maybe you would've stood a chance at becoming champion."

Coming from the man he'd rode and lived with for years, Shep felt like he'd been knocked on his ass. He knew he'd been a damn good bull rider, but that knowledge did little for his pride at that moment. God he wished he could compete, but with his knee the way it was...

Jeremy surprised him by stepping up to go toe to toe with his father. "I'm riding in the Cattle Valley Rodeo. If you think you're more a man than I am, prove it."

Todd looked over Jeremy's shoulder. "This your idea?" he asked Shep.

"No. But I support him whole heartedly, and I'll do anything in my power to help him," Shep answered, wrapping an arm around Jeremy's waist.

Todd's eyes narrowed as his lip curled in disgust. "You're fucking him," he stated.

"I'm in love with him," Shep replied.

Todd laughed and shook his head. "Come on, Regina. I can't stand the sight of these perverts another second."

Regina, who had been standing off to the side, wide-eyed, nodded and started to follow Todd. Before he opened the front door, Todd turned back around. "I should've known better. An old queen like you? Oh, how you used to love the young cowboy meat. Guess not much has changed, huh? Well, it sickened me then and it sickens me even more now."

Shep started to go after Todd once again, but Rance stepped between the two men. "Todd. If you don't get your ass off this property in the next thirty seconds, you'll never be able to ride again. I've got an entire ranch full of *fags* who I'm sure will be more than willing to teach you what a real man can do."

The threat must've finally gotten through, because Todd spun on his heels and walked out the door, suitcase in hand. He didn't even look back to make sure Regina was following.

As Shep watched him pull out of the drive, he shook his head. How could he have been so wrong about the kind of man Todd was? He felt like a fool.

Jeremy's arms wrapped around Shep's waist. "He's getting worse all the time."

"Is he? Or have I just always been blind to his true feelings about me?"

Jeremy shook his head. "I don't think so. I know he loved you as a friend when you lived with us. He couldn't have felt that way about you if he was disgusted with you being gay. No, I think something else might be going on."

"Doesn't excuse what he did to you," Shep said.

"No, it doesn't. I need to believe that he used to love me too, though," Jeremy whispered.

* * * *

The bell over the door jingled as Shep walked into Tyler's Floral and Gifts. He hadn't had a reason to stop into the fairly new shop since it had been remodelled. "Looks great in here," he commented, as Tyler came out from the back.

"Thanks," Tyler said, looking around his shop. "I doubted I'd ever see you in here. You must have a new man in your life."

Shep felt the blush creeping up his face. "Not really new, just finally acknowledged," he admitted.

He noticed a look of sadness steal over Tyler's face, before he quickly hid it. "What can I do for you?"

"Jeremy's riding in the rodeo in a few days. I wanted to get him something to let him know how proud I am of him."

Tyler rubbed his chin. "Like flowers or something else?"

"I don't know. Flowers will die and candy will be eaten. I was thinking something a little more permanent."

Tyler's brows shot up. "So this new relationship is serious?"

"As a heart attack." Shep looked around the store. "Do you have any rose bushes?"

"Yeah," Tyler continued to tap his chin. "You know, if it were me, and I wanted to show someone that I planned on a long life with them, I'd get a tree."

"A tree?" He hadn't thought of something as boring as a tree.

Tyler nodded and motioned for Shep to follow him. Shep stepped up to the counter and waited while Tyler dug out a book from the shelf behind him. "There are two varieties that I think you should consider. First is the American Linden, which has dark green heart-shaped leaves and grows up to around forty feet. In the early summer it has fragrant yellow blossoms. My second choice would be the Sensation Boxelder. It's a male variety so it won't attract the boxelder bugs. It's a very hardy tree and grows up to forty-feet as well."

Tyler turned the book around to show him the pictures. "In my opinion, nothing says longevity like a tree."

Shep studied the pictures. He thought of the side yard of the ranch house and the big empty space where lightning had struck the Bur Oak several years earlier. He could easily picture a new tree planted for Jeremy. "Do you have these here?"

"No, but I can either order you one, or you could run into Sheridan. I'm sure one of the greenhouses would carry them."

While Shep was trying to decide if he had time to run to Sheridan, the bell over the door announced another customer. Tyler leaned forward, whispering,

"Can you hold on? Hearn's here for the weekly bouquet he puts on Mitch's grave."

Shep nodded and waved at Hearn. The man looked absolutely miserable. Shep, along with most of the people in town, thought Mitch Lanham was an ass. Mitch had had a good man in Hearn, but the jerk was forever catting around with anyone who'd have him. Regardless, the man didn't deserve to die like he did, especially with both Hearn and Tyler in the car when it happened.

Deciding to give the two friends a bit of privacy, he went back to studying the book. He tried to imagine each tree in the spot he'd already picked out. A picture of him and Jeremy popped into his mind and his decision was made.

He turned towards Tyler to give him his decision and stopped. The look of love on Tyler's face as he handed the bouquet of white, yellow and pink daisies to Hearn was heartbreaking.

Hearn said something quietly and left the shop. Tyler stood, watching the door for several moments before turning back towards the counter. Shep flushed, knowing he'd just witnessed something extremely personal.

"Have you made a decision?" Tyler asked.

"Yeah. I really appreciate your help, but I think I'll run into Sheridan and pick up the American Linden if I can find it."

Tyler did his best to smile. "No problem. Your Jeremy is a very lucky man to have someone like you."

"No." Shep shook his head. "I'm the lucky one."

Carol Lynne

* * * *

By the time Shep pulled up to the ranch house, it was getting close to supper. He decided he'd wait until afterwards to surprise Jeremy with his gift. He got out and walked towards the bunkhouse.

Before he got there, Rance met him at the bottom of the steps and held up his hands. "I need to talk to you before you go in."

Shep looked over Rance's shoulder to the door and then back to his foreman. "Did something happen?" he asked, feeling his heart begin to beat faster.

"Yes and no. It's nothing serious, but I wanted you to know from me before you saw it for yourself."

"What?" Shep asked impatiently, trying to sidestep his friend.

"Jeremy landed hard on his hip earlier. Nothing's broken. It looks like it could just be a deep bruise, but he may have pulled a muscle."

Shep pushed Rance out of his way and burst through the door. "Where is he?"

"He insisted we take him to your house," Rance said from behind him. "Bo's with him, although Jeremy is putting up a fuss about it. He claims he's fine, but I noticed he was limping quite a bit."

"Thanks," Shep said, as he turned and sprinted towards the house.

He stepped inside the cool interior and looked in the living room. "Jeremy," he called out.

"Up here," Jeremy answered.

Shep ran up the stairs and into his bedroom. Jeremy was leaning against the headboard, playing cards with

Bo. His lover looked to be in fairly good spirits, although his lower half was covered by a sheet.

"How're you feeling?" Shep asked, going to Jeremy's side.

"Stupid," Jeremy answered.

Bo chose that moment to take the cards out of Jeremy's hand. He made a big production out of looking at them. "Damn, I would've beaten you, too. We'll play again some other time."

"You're on," Jeremy chuckled. "Thanks for babysitting."

Bo chuckled. "At least I didn't have to powder your ass and change your diapers."

"Good thing," Shep grunted.

Laughing, Bo waved and left the room. As soon as he heard the front door open and close, Shep pealed back the sheet. "Fuck," he spat out. The livid purple and blue bruise went from Jeremy's hip, towards his groin and down his thigh.

Jeremy tried to wrestle the sheet away from him. "It's nothing. We put some salve on it. Hopefully it'll be better by morning."

Shep leaned over Jeremy and rubbed his nose against his lover's. "Who put salve on it?" The thought of Bo rubbing his hands over Jeremy's nude body wasn't sitting well.

"I did most of it, but Bo helped me with the places I couldn't reach." Jeremy cupped Shep's cheeks and laughed. "Believe me. I was in no mood to enjoy it."

Shep began to undress, but stopped. "Do you need anything to eat before I crawl in with you?"

Jeremy shook his head. "All I need is you."

Now nude, Shep gently climbed under the sheet and pressed himself against Jeremy's uninjured side. He thought briefly about the tree in the back of the truck, but decided to wait until morning to give Jeremy his present.

As his lover snuggled against him and started to doze, Shep looked out the window and smiled. Some day they'd be able to lie right here and see their tree out that same window.

His mind began to wonder if Jeremy riding was such a good idea. He thought of the look on Hearn's face. Was it worth the chance?

Chapter Ten

"Hey," Shep said, finding Rance in the arena. "I poked a pain pill down Jeremy's throat and told him to sleep the rest of the day. If you need help with anything, I'll be around in a couple of hours. First I'm going into town to make sure Todd's registered for the rodeo."

Rance nodded. "You want one of the boys to plant that tree I saw leaning against the house?"

"Nope. That's a present for Jeremy. I'll plant it when I get back."

Rance grinned. "I think I'll sell tickets. I doubt there's a single man here who's seen you do the kind of work digging that hole is gonna require."

"Shut up, smartass. There's a reason I'm the boss," Shep answered with his own grin.

Rance was still laughing as Shep got into his truck.

He worried about Jeremy as he drove the four miles into town. He knew Jeremy would be able to ride, despite his hip. Hell, he'd done it himself a dozen times over the years, but he also knew how painful it would be.

Shep had spent almost an hour trying to talk Jeremy out of competing, but his lover would listen to none of it. Insisting once again it was the only way to gain respect in his father's eyes. Shep knew Jeremy could win a hundred competitions and never earn the respect of a man like Todd, but he kept his mouth shut. If nothing else, it would be good for Todd to learn a little humility at the hands of his son.

Parking in front of city hall, Shep went straight to Carol's office. Although the door was open, he politely knocked on the threshold.

Carol looked up from her computer. "Hi, Shep. Quade isn't in right now."

Shep took off his cowboy hat and stepped into the small outer office. "Hi, Carol. I came to ask a favour if you don't mind."

The middle-aged secretary took off her glasses and eyed him. "That would depend on what kind of a favour, now wouldn't it?"

He grinned. "Yes, ma'am. I was wondering if you could tell me whether Todd Lovell has registered to ride this weekend?"

One of Carol's dark brown eyebrows shot up. "Shepard Black. Do I look older than you? Everyone knows you don't call a woman ma'am unless she's at least got grey hair. Do you see any grey hair on this head?"

He shook his head. "No. I'm sorry. I didn't mean any offence."

Carol sighed and rolled her eyes, tossing her glasses onto the desk. "You didn't. I'm the one who should be sorry. It's been a bad week around here. Sorry if I tried to take it out on you."

"The big twenty-fifth anniversary running you ragged is it?"

"Oh hell no. I could handle that stuff with my eyes closed. No, it's Quade. He's driving me absolutely nuts."

The relationship between the mayor and his secretary was legendary. The two of them constantly fought like husband and wife, but deep down anyone could tell they honestly cared about each other. "What's Quade doing now?"

"Not a damn thing. That's the problem. Ever since he got back from Hawaii he's done nothing but mope around. I thought the new lodge going in up the mountain would light a fire under his ass, but even that didn't do it."

"He'll find his way eventually. I know that doesn't help much. You're the one who has to work with him day in and day out, but it will get better."

"Humpf." Carol picked her glasses back up and slid them on. "To answer your question, no, Mr. Lovell hasn't been in to register. Of course he may be waiting to do it the morning of the rodeo."

"Thanks," Shep said, and waved as he walked out of the office.

After stopping by the rodeo arena just outside of town, Shep headed his truck towards Sheridan. He'd been lucky enough to catch a friend of Todd's unloading his horse. Jim told him he'd received a call from Todd and he and Regina were staying in the city an hour north of Cattle Valley.

Looking at Todd's truck parked in front of the single story motel, he gripped the steering wheel. Talking to Todd was the last thing on earth he felt like doing, but this wasn't about him. He'd told Jeremy point blank that he'd get a chance to compete against his father, and by God, Shep was going to make sure it happened.

With new resolve, he got out of the truck and went to the door directly in front of Todd's truck. He pounded for several minutes before he started yelling. "Todd! Open up!"

Finally, the door two down from him opened and Todd stepped out. "What the hell do you want now?"

Shep turned and stalked towards his ex-friend. "I wanna know why you haven't registered for the rodeo?"

"Decided against it. I won't be part of some grudge match from my own son."

Todd talked a good game, but Shep was beginning to see through the façade. *He knows he's going to lose*, he thought. "You'll ride," Shep stated. "Because if you don't, the press will get a call. What do you think your many fans would think if they learned the great Todd Lovell physically abused his own son?"

"You wouldn't dare," Todd growled.

"Try me." Shep spun and walked back to his truck. "I'll expect to see you on Friday at the qualifiers," he casually said over his shoulder.

* * * *

Jeremy woke with a cool wet body leaning over him. "Hey," he said and pulled Shep's head down for a kiss. "You just get home?"

"Nope," Shep replied. "Been home a couple of hours. I was pretty gross so I thought I'd come up and ask you to join me in a shower, but you were sound asleep." Shep settled beside him on the bed.

"You should've woken me up. I need a shower anyway. I've done nothing but lay in this bed since the fall and I'm getting pretty rank," he said, with a sniff to his underarms.

"Mmm," Shep moaned, sticking his nose in Jeremy's arm pit. "You smell like a man to me."

"Yeah? Then why did you shower off your manly smell?" He circled Shep's nipple with his finger, watching as it pebbled.

"Cuz I was dirty, not just sweaty."

Dirty? Shep? "What, were the ledgers dusty?"

"Very funny. I think you and Rance must've gone to the same clown school."

Even though Shep chuckled, Jeremy could see that his words had wounded his pride. He placed a kiss on Shep's neck. "I'm sorry. It's just that lately I'm not used to seeing you work outside of your office."

Shep sighed and ran his hand down Jeremy's back. "It's the only part about this place that I hate."

"So hire someone else to do the books," Jeremy offered.

"I could do that, but then what would I do?" Shep shifted uncomfortably until he was lying on his side facing Jeremy. "My knee's fine for the most part, but after a couple of hours on my feet it starts throbbing. I've found it easier to not let employees see their boss in pain. No sense in proving to them that I'm a washed up ex-bull rider."

Jeremy sat up, wincing when he moved too fast. "You've done things the men on this ranch can only dream about, so don't give me the 'poor me' routine. Besides, we're more than your employees, we're your friends."

Shep pulled him back down to his side. "Calm down there, buckaroo."

"I'm just sayin'."

"I know what you're saying, and I agree. I am surrounded by friends."

Jeremy settled in and ran his hand down Shep's chest to cup his balls. "Maybe you could give Rance and Bo a few more duties?"

"Like what?" Shep asked.

"Well. Make Bo keep all the books on the feed and hay inventory. He's really smart and he did something similar at that commune he used to live at. And Rance is more than capable of entering his own breeding data into the computer. Even if you only manage to free up a couple of hours a day, I think it'll make you feel better."

Jeremy held his breath. He needed Shep to take him seriously. Not only would it bode well for their future relationship, but he suddenly felt afraid. What if Shep decided ranching wasn't for him and sold the place?

Shep was still working things out in his mind it appeared. Jeremy gave his lover's balls a gentle squeeze. "Please don't get bored and leave me," he whispered.

Shep's unblinking gaze went from the blank wall, to Jeremy. "What? Why would I get bored and leave you? Haven't you figured out by now that you're the most important thing in my life?"

Shep blew out a frustrated breath and sat up. "Come on. Get dressed. I've something I want to show you."

More than a little confused, Jeremy sat up. He stood without allowing his face to betray the amount of pain he was in. He looked around the room. "Where're my jeans?"

"Wash. Sorry, I forgot about them. I'll toss them in the dryer when we go down," Shep said. He walked over and dug a pair of sweats out of his dresser. "Put these on for now."

Jeremy caught the faded navy sweats and sat back down on the bed to put them on. When he stood, the pants fell down his waist to ride low on his hips. He looked down at the short patch of pubic hair exposed. "You really want me to go around like this?"

"Fuck," Shep said and went to his knees in front of Jeremy. Burying his face in Jeremy's crotch, Shep groaned.

Jeremy moaned as Shep mouthed his quickly filling cock through the soft sweats. He reached down and braced his hands on the wide shoulders in front of him. Shep nudged the sweats further down with his chin and took Jeremy's cock into his mouth.

"Oh, god," Jeremy moaned and thrust towards Shep's face.

His lover enthusiastically sucked and licked his cock. It was pure heaven until Shep tried to anchor himself against Jeremy's thrusts by gripping his hips.

The hiss of pain erupted from his throat before he could swallow it. Shep immediately dropped his hands and let Jeremy's quickly deflating cock slip from his lips.

"Oh, sweetheart, I'm so sorry," Shep said. He stood and wrapped his arms around Jeremy. "I wouldn't hurt you for anything in the world."

He snuggled against Shep's chest. "I know that. We both just got a little carried away. Believe me, with you sucking my cock, the last thing on my mind was going easy on my hip."

Shep looked into Jeremy's eyes for several seconds before closing the distance. He ran his tongue around Jeremy's lips, before delving inside. Jeremy could taste his own flavour on his lover's tongue.

He pulled back and grinned. "What was it that you wanted to show me?"

"Oh. Oh! Yeah, come on." Shep led him by the hand out of the bedroom and down the stairs. "Wrap a hand around the waistband of those pants, cuz we're going outside. I'd hate to have to poke the eyes out of one of my cowboys for gawking at you."

He loved it when Shep got all jealous and protective. He'd had nothing but time to think for the previous day and a half and his dad's words kept coming back to him. He really hoped Todd was wrong and Shep saw more in him than just a young cowboy to fuck. In his heart, he knew that the words were only meant to hurt both of them, but it was definitely something he'd thought about. Hell, the young gay guys that hung around the circuit still asked about Shep and if he was ever going to come back to visit.

Shep led him around the side of the house and stopped. Jeremy was pulled into the big cowboy's arms. "I wanted to get you something special to let you know how proud I am of you." Shep kissed him before stepping back and gesturing towards the freshly planted eight foot tree.

"You planted that?" He was a little confused by the gift, but the fact that Shep had given him anything filled him with joy.

"Yeah. It's an American Linden, called Legend. Come here, I wanna show you something." Shep pulled Jeremy forward and plucked one of the dark green leaves off the tree. "See the leaves? They're heart-shaped. The way I see it, by the time this little guy is forty feet tall, it'll be covered with 'I love yous'."

Jeremy had never heard anything more beautiful. He felt the sting of tears as Shep continued.

"In about ten years or so, we'll be able to lie in bed and watch the leaves blow in the breeze. I thought maybe I'd build some kind of patio under it once it gets tall enough. Maybe put a wide chaise lounge on it. Of course it would have to be big enough for the two of us."

"Stop," Jeremy said, moments before he kissed the man he loved. He poured every ounce of his feelings into that one kiss. Breaking away, he looked into Shep's blue eyes. "It's the best gift you could've given me." All the worries brought on by his dad's cruel words vanished in an instant.

"Hey. What's wrong?" Shep asked, wiping the tear that trickled down Jeremy's face.

"Nothing. I'm glad you see us together ten years down the road."

"Ten?" Shep laughed. "That's just the beginning."

Chapter Eleven

"Morning," Shep said, sipping coffee from his insulated mug.

"Morning," Rance returned. "We're getting ready to load the stock for the rodeo. I figure we can do it in three trips."

Shep nodded and yawned. "Sounds good." He studied the bulls. They were agitated this morning. It was obvious by their demeanour they knew something was about to happen. "Who else do you have helping?"

"Buddy's hooking up the trailer as we speak. I also have Jim and Steve finishing up their chores so they can lend a hand."

"And Bo?" Shep asked.

"In the hayfield as usual. He seems to think a storm is on its way and he wants to get the hay on the ground bailed before the rodeo."

Shep looked up and shrugged. "Well, the sky's blue as can be, and my knee isn't bugging me, so I think he's wrong."

"Who knows. Where's Jeremy? Is he up to the qualifiers later?"

"Says he is. I've been rubbing him down with liniment about five times a day. He's trying to figure out what to wear," Shep chuckled. "He's nervous as hell and twice as cute."

Rance chuckled. "I'll take your word for it."

Buddy pulled around the side of the equipment shed and backed the trailer up to the stock pens. "Let's start with the bulls. I don't like the way they're looking at me."

For the next thirty minutes they loaded the agitated animals. He was just closing the trailer gate when Jeremy walked up behind him.

"Hey. Sorry I wasn't down quick enough to help," Jeremy chuckled.

Distracted, Shep released his grip on the gate long enough for Hell's Bells to head butt the piece of metal. The heavy gate banged into Shep's injured knee, eliciting a cry of pain.

Jeremy and Rance rushed forward, pushing the gate closed and locking it. Shep bent over, afraid he was going to throw up from the searing pain. Jeremy tried to touch him, but Shep held up his hand, silently asking for a moment to himself. It had been several years since he'd experienced this level of pain. *I'm getting soft.*

After spitting several times into the dirt, Shep balanced his weight on one leg and stood. "Will you help me to the truck?" he asked Jeremy.

"No," Jeremy said. "But I'll go get your pickup and help you into that." He took off before Shep could object.

"You need to get to the doctor," Rance said, putting a steadying arm around Shep's waist.

"I'll be fine," he argued. "I just need to sit down for a few minutes."

"With as much hardware as that knee is packing, something could've easily been knocked loose. Just shut up and let us take care of you."

Great. That's all I need. He'd promised Jeremy he'd dance with him at the street celebration after the rodeo.

His truck pulled up directly in front of him and Jeremy hopped out. Common sense and pain overrode any further argument he was prepared to give. He let Rance and Jeremy help him into the truck. "Get those bulls to the arena," he said to Rance, as Jeremy climbed into the driver's seat.

He put his seat back as far as it would go and stretched out his leg, wincing every time they hit a bump in the road. "I'm getting old," he mumbled.

Jeremy reached over and gripped his hand. "No you're not. You just got distracted by my amazingly sexy body."

"I believe that. Of course it'll be your own fault if I can't keep my promise to dance with you."

Jeremy chuckled. "We make quite a pair. Two lame cowboys with a huge weekend in front of us."

By the time they pulled up to the back emergency entrance, the pain in Shep's knee had eased a bit. Still, he didn't put up a fuss when Jeremy went to find a wheelchair. A smiling face popped through his open window.

"I hear you had some trouble," Dr. Singer said.

Shep rolled his eyes. He really wasn't in the mood for Isaac's cheerfulness. Of course the man had two times the reason to be happy these days. He spotted Matt pushing a wheelchair out of the entrance with Jeremy in tow.

"Here we go," Matt said and locked the breaks on the chair. "Let's get you inside."

Isaac and Matt helped him out of the truck, as Jeremy hovered nearby. He reached out and took his lover's hand. "Shouldn't you be getting ready to ride?"

Jeremy shook his head. "Like I could concentrate with you in here. Give me a break."

Isaac wheeled him into an exam room and Matt knelt in front of him. He felt Shep's knee through the denim before shaking his head. "Sorry, these need to come off. Can you do it, or do you want me to cut them off?"

"Are you kiddin'. They may be faded, but these are perfectly good jeans." Shep unzipped his fly. "Want to help me?" he asked with a wink to Jeremy.

Jeremy gripped the waistband, as Shep levered himself up using the arms of the wheelchair. His lover easily slipped the denim down and off, paying close attention not to jostle his knee.

Matt whistled as he looked at the roadmap of scars decorating his left leg. "Damn. You've had a little work done, haven't you?"

"A little over four years ago. They had to reconstruct the damn thing using chicken wire and super glue."

Matt chuckled. "Whatever works." The young physical therapist began examining Shep's knee, manipulating it this way and that way. He finally eased it back down. "I'd like an x-ray, but my guess is it's probably just a deep contusion." Matt looked up at Isaac. "You want to do the honours?"

"Might as well. I don't have a scheduled appointment for another hour." He stood behind Shep's wheelchair. "Come on, cowboy. Let's go take a ride on the x-ray table."

Shep looked over at Jeremy and rolled his eyes.

* * * *

It took another hour before Shep and Jeremy were on their way. "You sure you don't want me to take you home?" Jeremy asked. "I've got plenty of time to get there and back to the arena."

Shep shook his head, no. Matt had given him a couple of low dosage pain pills and they were making him a little drowsy. "I might sleep a few minutes in the truck before you ride, but I don't want to miss it."

He thought of something Isaac had mentioned in passing. Evidently the doctor hadn't gotten the word that Todd was no longer his best friend. "Isaac said your dad came in for a refill of his pain meds." He looked over at Jeremy. "Did you know he was taking them?"

Jeremy's brows shot up. "No. I had no idea. Did Doc say what they were for?"

"Joint pain. Most likely he's having the onset of arthritis, too many broken body parts, I guess." He couldn't help but to wonder whether his changed personality was due to pain, or the medicine. Maybe neither. Perhaps it was the knowledge he wouldn't be able to ride much longer. He started to say something to Jeremy but stopped himself. The last thing Jeremy needed was to worry about Todd right before he rode.

"Sure you're ready for this?" Shep asked. "It's been several days since you've practiced."

Jeremy leaned over the low console and kissed him. "I'm sure. I've been practicing for this day since I was thirteen years old," Jeremy reminded him before taking off across the parking lot.

Shep was just getting comfortable again, when Rance strolled up to the truck and knocked on the hood. "How's the knee?"

Shep looked down at the black Velcro wrap around his leg. "Okay. Sore, but nothing seems out of place. Did you bring Jeremy's rigging?"

"Yeah. It's in the cab of the truck." Rance looked like he wanted to say something else.

"What?" Shep finally asked after a few moments.

"Todd's here. Been talking some smack about you and Jeremy."

The first thing Shep thought of was Jeremy's safety. He knew in his present condition he wouldn't be much help in a fight. "Do me a favour and keep your eyes on Jeremy. Todd has a pretty good track record of making sure Jeremy doesn't compete against him."

Rance narrowed his eyes. "I know about the cut on his face. What aren't you telling me?"

Shep went on to tell his foreman about Todd breaking Jeremy's ribs the last time he'd tried to ride. "Sonofabitch," Rance cussed, and spit on the ground.

"I imagine Bo's caught up to Jeremy by now, but I'll go keep an eye on both of them."

Shep grinned and winked at his loyal friend. "You do that. Just make sure your eyes aren't looking below the waist," he said with a chuckle.

Blowing out a disgusted breath, Rance turned and walked towards the arena. Shep rubbed his jaw in thought. Rance had come to the ranch shortly after Shep had bought the place. He told Shep he'd grown up on a ranch, but had moved to Boston to pursue a career in law enforcement. Then Rance had told him a secret. One that Shep would take to his grave.

He'd had several discussions with his friend over the years. In the dead of winter, there was a lot more downtime on a ranch. He and Rance would get drunk in front of the fire and discuss life and what they both wanted out of it. It broke Shep's heart every time to hear Rance say he knew he'd die alone and he'd accepted it.

Watching the broad back of his foreman walk away, Shep hated the man's decision. Bo clearly wanted to get to know Rance, but the man shut him out at every available opportunity. Although Shep knew he couldn't give up the man's secret, maybe he could make it a little harder on his friend to resist Bo's overtures.

His eyes drifted shut with a plan in mind, one that would not only help him, but Rance and Bo as well.

* * * *

"Hey. I thought you'd never get here," Bo said, running up to him.

"Couldn't be helped. I had to make sure my man was okay," Jeremy said with a grin.

Bo grinned back. "I can understand that."

Jeremy noticed Bo looking around. "I saw him walking towards the truck as I was coming in."

"Who?" Bo asked.

Jeremy smiled at the innocent look on Bo's face. "Rance. Who else would you be looking for?"

Bo shook his head. "Actually, you're wrong. I was looking for Todd. Rance asked me to keep an eye on him."

He quickly scanned the surrounding crowd. Riders and early fans were everywhere. "Do you see him?" The twist of fear that shot through him was ridiculous, he knew it, but couldn't do much about it.

Bo pointed towards the small grand stand. "He's signing autographs for his adoring public," Bo said with a sneer.

"I need to go pick up my number. Did you bring my stuff?"

"Yeah it's in the truck. We can get it after you check in."

Bo walked beside him to the shaded area under the stands where the sign-in table had been set up. While they waited in line, Bo never got more than a foot away from him. For some reason it tickled him. He was probably the only rider in attendance who had a bodyguard.

After signing in and getting his number, Jeremy moved to the side and handed it to his friend along with two safety pins. "Mind putting this on for me?"

As Bo was pinning it on, Jeremy heard a familiar voice behind him. "So you're really going to do this,"

Todd laughed. "Prepare to be embarrassed in front of a thousand people."

"Get lost," Bo growled finishing the task at hand.

"So you've replaced Shep already? Don't blame you, boy. He would've gotten tired of you before long anyway. That's the thing with Shep. He's only interested in the thrill of the conquest, after that he gets bored."

Jeremy tried not to let the words get to him. He knew his dad was only trying to rattle him before his ride. The problem was, he'd worried about that very thing since he and Shep had gotten together. His mouth overruled his brain. "No, Dad. That's more your style." He looked around. "I don't see Regina. Oh, that's right. I did see Trick Allen's tour bus as we passed through town. What? She on to bigger and brighter stars?"

"You little faggot," Todd spat out.

"Walk away," Bo whispered in his ear. "We're starting to gather a crowd. It'll look worse for Todd if you just ignore him after what he just said. Don't forget, he's surrounded by faggots."

Jeremy nodded. He'd happily walk away, not as much to punish his dad, but because he didn't know what to say in return. He let Bo lead him out of the shade and to the stockyard.

"The truck's parked over here. We'll get your gear and keep you away from Todd until it's time for you to ride."

Jeremy knew he needed a quiet place to gather his concentration. After retrieving his things, he sat on the ground in the shade of the trailer. "I'm gonna need some time to myself," he told Bo.

His friend's eyes narrowed as he studied the surroundings. "I'll go just down there. Far enough away to give you peace, but close enough to watch your back."

Jeremy smiled. "Thanks, tough man."

Bo chuckled and walked off.

Pulling his bag of gear closer, Jeremy made sure he had everything he'd need. While he was at it, he went ahead and put on his chaps and spurs. The protective vest he always wore could wait, along with his glove.

Staring down at the bull rope in his hands, he pictured his ride, over and over. He tried to remember and go through every trick Shep had taught him to impress the judges. His first round would be on a bull he'd never ridden but had heard about. One of a truckload brought in from Cheyenne, Zero Tolerance, was supposed to be a hell of a ride. Jeremy just hoped he didn't end up making a fool of not only himself, but Shep as well.

Chapter Twelve

"You shouldn't be walking around," Jeremy said.

"How else was I gonna get over here?" Shep tried to joke. Sobering, he reached out and brushed Jeremy's cheek with his knuckles.

Jeremy must've read his mind. "I can do this."

Shep nodded. He wanted to pull his lover into his arms and keep him safe from the two thousand pound bull, but he stepped back instead. Jeremy needed every ounce of concentration to keep himself safe, and Shep would do nothing to jeopardise him.

He leaned against the railing and watched as Jeremy's cute little ass framed by an old pair of chaps, walked to the chute. Bo and Rance flanked Jeremy, Bo carrying the bull rope, cow bell jangling.

Shep's gut was in knots as they prepared Jeremy and the bull for the first ride of the day. In a way he was glad that Jeremy was up first. It would mean less time for nerves to set in and less time for Todd to try and fuck with his son's head.

He'd already been told about the run-in under the grandstand from Rance, who'd heard it from Bo. He walked closer to get a better look at Jeremy's ride. The scene was so familiar it took him back in time for a few minutes. There was something about the smell of popcorn and cotton candy. Shep chuckled. He'd never understood cotton candy, especially at a dusty fair or rodeo event. Perhaps people merely held the pink glob of spun sugar in front of their mouths to filter out the dirt in the air kicked up by bull and rider.

The paid announcer introduced Jeremy to the crowd. Shep's gut twisted further. So many things could go wrong in eight seconds. He watched as Jeremy wrapped the bull rope around his hand, adjusting the fit until it was just right. A subtle nod of his cowboy hat and the gate opened.

The crowd went wild as Zero Tolerance bucked and spun his way in circles. Jeremy held onto the bull rope with one hand as the other moved back and forth in the air. When the eight second buzzer sounded, Shep was finally able to release the breath he'd been holding.

Jeremy should've earned a decent score with that ride. The judges scores came up, eighty point seven five. He'd need to add a little more finesse in the finals to win, but at least he had a good shot of moving on to the next round.

His heart didn't start beating normally again until Jeremy was out of the arena and walking towards him, silly grin plastered on his face. "Ya did good," Shep said. He opened his arms and Jeremy walked right into them.

"Thanks," Jeremy said. "It felt pretty good. I know I didn't pull out all the stops, but I thought I'd save something to shock them with later."

Shep looked into Jeremy's brown eyes and grinned. "Let's just worry about one ride at a time."

A disturbance off to the right drew their attention.

"Fuck you, Jax. You aren't my boss today," the good-looking man said.

Shep whispered in Jeremy's ear. "You know that guy?"

"He's the new cowboy at the EZ Does It. Came down from Montana to replace Smokey," Jeremy whispered back.

Shep watched as Jax Brolin got right in Logan's face. With the number pinned to the back of Logan's shirt, it was obvious the guy was planning to ride. Evidently, Jax wasn't happy about it. "You don't know what the hell you're doing. And it will be my business when you break your fucking neck, and I have to replace your ass come Monday."

Logan backed Jax up against one of the steel rails. "What? You're the one who goaded me into doing it, and now you change your mind? I don't think so. I may be a lot of things, but yella isn't one of them." Logan stomped off, with Jax right on his heels.

"They together?" Shep asked Jeremy.

Jeremy shrugged. Todd's name was announced over the loud speaker to much fanfare. Jeremy turned towards the arena. "Mind if we watch?"

Shep shook his head. "As long you don't let him psych you out."

"I won't."

Jeremy helped Shep move close enough to see the ride in better detail. "Did you watch me from all the way back there?"

"Yep." Shep felt his face flush. "I was a bit nervous," he admitted.

Shep watched Todd settle on the back of the bull. The second the gate opened, Shep studied his old friend. There was definitely something different. He hadn't seen Todd ride in a couple of years, and it appeared age was catching up to the champion.

Todd managed to hang on the whole eight seconds before he jumped off and was quickly up and over the fence. Shep waited for the judge's scores, eighty-three point five. He shook his head, knowing the judge's scores were too high. "They scored him on who he is instead of how he rode," he commented.

Jeremy shrugged beside him. "It is what it is."

The odd tone of his lover's voice caught his attention. Wrapping his arm tighter around Jeremy's stomach, he kissed the side of his neck. "You okay?"

"Yeah," Jeremy said without turning towards him. "Logan's up."

Shep turned his attention back to the action in the arena. He shook his head as Logan managed to stay on the bull for the full eight seconds. "That was the nastiest eight seconds I've ever witnessed," he chuckled.

The way Logan's muscles strained against the tight confines of his T-shirt, Shep guessed it was brute strength and a hell of a lot of luck. He smiled as Jax was right there and in Logan's face again as soon as the younger man hopped over the fence.

"I need to get ready for my next ride," Jeremy said.

Shep nodded. He knew all about needing space to get your head together. Leading Jeremy over to the side, he gently placed him in the shadows and stood in front of him. "You do your thing, and I'll make sure no one bothers ya."

He felt a touch to his back. "Thanks," Jeremy said.

* * * *

Jeremy was sound asleep before they even made it out of the parking lot. He'd done what he'd set out to do. He hadn't come in first or second in the preliminaries, but at least he made it to the finals.

His plan was to get his cowboy home, fed and then a nice long massage was in order. As he drove, he couldn't get Todd off his mind. His ex-friend had come in first, naturally, but he hadn't really earned it. Shep decided to do some research when they got home. Once he saw to the needs of his cowboy.

Pulling up to the house, Shep reached over and brushed a hand down Jeremy's stomach. "Wake up, sleepyhead. We're home, and I'm in no shape to carry you."

Jeremy's eyes blinked rapidly before they finally opened. "Damn. Can't you drive around for another couple of hours?" he asked with a devilish grin.

"Come on. Roll your young bones out of the truck and up the stairs." Shep got out and hobbled his way around the truck. He opened Jeremy's door and grinned. In the time it had taken him to come around, Jeremy had already fallen back into a doze.

Shep loved his cowboy enough to consider doing what Jeremy had asked, and drive him around for a few hours. The ranch truck pulling down the drive gave him another option. He held up his hand, signalling for Rance to stop.

His foreman rolled down the driver's window. "Problem?"

"Yeah," Shep chuckled. Putting jealousy aside, he asked for what would be best for Jeremy. "Bo, can you help me get Jeremy upstairs? I can't seem to rouse him enough for him to make it on his own."

Laughing, Bo jumped out of the passenger seat and walked over, giving Rance a wave to go on without him. With his hands on his hips, Bo studied the sleeping bull rider. "Want me to just carry him up?"

"If you think you can."

Bo started to reach for Jeremy, but Shep reached out and stopped him. "Just carry him. No free feels."

Bo chuckled and nodded. "I promise, Boss. I got my sights set on another cowboy anyway."

Shep's gut clenched. Even though Bo said it in a light hearted fashion, Shep could hear the feelings behind the word. He vowed once again to do something to bring Rance around. He watched as Bo carefully lifted Jeremy from the seat. As Bo turned towards the house, Jeremy readjusted and wrapped his arms around Bo's neck, snuggling into his chest.

"Woa there, buddy. You trying to get me killed?" Bo joked.

Still sound asleep, Jeremy didn't even acknowledge Bo's remark. Shep pointed towards the house and Bo carried Jeremy up the steps and inside. "I guess you want him upstairs."

"Yeah, if you think you can carry him that far. He might not weigh that much, but he's a tall one," Shep said. "I'm gonna make a couple of sandwiches. You want one?" Now why did he ask that?

"Sure. I'll be down shortly. I'll leave the undressing for you."

"You'd better," Shep grunted. He made his way into the kitchen and started pulling out lunch meat. Why had he asked Bo to stay for something to eat? Maybe the sadness in the ranch hand's voice had something to do with it. He knew he couldn't divulge Rance's secrets, but maybe he could shed some light on why his foreman acted the way he did. If nothing else, it would buy some time until he got his plan into place.

Within minutes Bo was striding into the kitchen. "I don't think he ever woke up."

Bo took a seat at the kitchen table as Shep set a plate down in front of him. "You want a beer?" Shep asked.

"Sure," Bo replied.

After getting out two cans, Shep took a seat. He decided to jump right in to the conversation. "Jeremy and I were talking, and I'd like to free up some time out of the office. Jeremy suggested that you might be interested in entering your own feed data into the computer."

"I can do that," Bo said, swallowing a bite of sandwich.

"Good. I'm gonna talk to Rance about letting him take over some of the computer work as well. I thought I'd get one installed for the two of you to share, but I don't think the office in the arena is a good place, too dusty. I'm considering just putting it in Rance's cabin. Would that be a problem for you?"

Bo grinned and shook his head. "Not at all. Of course Rance might have other ideas. It seems he does everything he can to keep his distance from me. I guess we could work out a schedule though."

Okay, here it comes. "Be patient with him. He's got more baggage than a normal man is forced to carry."

One of Bo's black eyebrows shot up. "More than me?"

"Depends on your definition. The big difference between the two of you is that you've learned to live with your baggage. Rance hasn't." There. That's all he was gonna say on the matter. "Speaking of which, how's your health?" The last thing he needed was to get the two of them together and see his foreman's heart broken if something were to happen to Bo.

"Good. I've lived with HIV for years. I know how to take care of myself."

Shep nodded. That's just what he needed to hear. The two of them ate the rest of their meal in companionable silence. When the last of the food was gone, Shep rose to his feet. "Well, I'm gonna go up and take a shower. I feel like I'm covered with at least two inches of dust."

"Thanks for the food," Bo said and stood to leave.

Before Bo walked out the back door, Shep called out. "Remember. Plant the seeds and give them time to grow before you attempt a harvest."

Bo turned back and looked into Shep's eyes for several moments before nodding. "I'll do that. Thanks, Boss."

"It's Shep. And you're welcome."

* * * *

Jeremy opened his eyes and stretched, wincing as his sore muscles protested the movement. Today was the day. He turned his head to the side and watched Shep sleep as he went over his ride time and time again.

The more he went over things, the more unease he felt. Watching his dad ride in the preliminaries had really opened his eyes. He had no doubts the old man could be beat if he put his mind to it, but at what cost?

Shep stirred and Jeremy watched those bright blue eyes focus on him. "Hey," Shep mumbled sleepily. "How're you feeling?"

"Okay. A little stiff, but I'm sure it's nothing that we can't work out with a little pre-ride activity," Jeremy said with a wink. He hadn't had his lover inside of him for almost two days and his ass was feeling neglected.

Shep reached out and hauled Jeremy on top of him, being mindful of his injured knee. Jeremy nipped and laved Shep's clavicle and worked his way up to those soft lips he loved so much. Their tongues duelled in a passionate kiss.

"Love you," Shep whispered, when they came up for air.

"I love you, too," Jeremy answered. He could feel Shep's cock hard and wet against his stomach. Smiling, he reached between them and took the fat erection into his fist. "You're my favourite bull. Wanna ride you."

Shep reached over to the nightstand and grabbed the bottle of lube. "You sure? I'd imagine your ass would already be pretty sore. Sure you want to add to it?"

Jeremy answered by moving to Shep's side as he turned himself to face the foot of the bed, presenting his ass like a gift. "I want to be able to feel your cock in me for the rest of the day, so don't expect anything slow and loving. I want a fuck to remember."

Shep's lubed fingers traced the ridged skin around his hole. "Well, with my knee the way it is, you'll be the one doing most of the work. Guess I don't have much say in the pace you set."

"You always have a say," Jeremy reminded him. "I'm just hoping your desires are the same as mine." He groaned as Shep pushed his thumb past the first ring of muscles. Oh yeah, they seemed of like minds as Shep quickly withdrew his thumb and inserted two fingers in its place.

"Oh god," Jeremy moaned, pushing back against those wonderfully thick digits. "Enough," he suddenly said.

Turning around, he straddled Shep's lap, as his lover used the time to run a slick hand up and down his cock. Shep held the thick shaft by the base as Jeremy slowly impaled himself, the burn, the stretch, sending shivers up his spine. Goosebumps rose on his arms and legs as he seated himself fully, his ass resting against Shep's balls.

His legs tried to protest as he began moving up and down on Shep's cock. Jeremy quickly pushed aside the call of his aching muscles and picked up speed. Every downward motion was sheer ecstasy.

When Shep reached out and wrapped his fingers around Jeremy's bobbing erection, a loud moan erupted from his throat. "Not gonna take long," he grunted.

Shep began to thrust up, pushing his cock even deeper into Jeremy's body.

Sweat dripped from Jeremy's forehead, landing in small puddles on Shep's hairy chest. On the next downward plunge, Jeremy's hips did a little figure eight, grinding himself against his lover.

Shep moaned and pressed a thumb to the slit of Jeremy's cock. Looking down, Jeremy watched as the first spurt of seed erupted, coating that big tanned digit. "Fuck," he shouted. He'd wanted to hold out longer, but between the big cock filling his ass and Shep's talented hand it was a lost cause.

Jeremy managed to keep his eyes open long enough to watch another jet of cum paint Shep's chest. Jeremy leaned forward and lapped his own essence off his man's chest. The sight must've done something for Shep, because Jeremy's ass was clasped in a brutal grip as his lover's body vibrated under him.

Falling completely against Shep's chest, Jeremy fought for each breath. *Oh yeah, I'm definitely going to feel Shep's cock for the rest of the day.*

Chapter Thirteen

The first thing Jeremy saw as he stepped out of the truck, was his dad surrounded by fans. He chuckled. The majority of the crowd appeared to be women, most of them blonde and stacked. It amazed him. His dad was fair looking, but definitely nothing that would draw a second glance from the women had he not been wearing that World Champion belt buckle. Sad really.

Shep stepped up beside him and followed his gaze. "He'll never change. Lose one, get another."

Jeremy looked from his dad to Shep. "You suppose it gets lonely? I mean, yeah he has sex regularly, but he has to know it'll all dry up some day."

Shep's eyes seemed to study him for several moments. "It's the life he's cultivated. I don't think Todd even looks towards the future. He's too busy living in the glory of the present."

The image of his dad's rides the previous day flashed through Jeremy's mind. It appeared the World Champion needed to rethink that plan.

Shep turned and pulled Jeremy's gear bag out of the back of the truck. "Let's find a shady spot."

He could tell by the tone of Shep's voice that something was going on. Instead of demanding to know what it was, he let the man he loved lead him to one of the several trees sprinkled around.

Once they were settled together under a big cottonwood, Jeremy took Shep's hand. "You noticed it, didn't you?"

"Noticed what, sweetheart?" Shep asked.

"Dad's losing it."

Shep exhaled and nodded. "I did a little research before I came to bed. Todd didn't opt out of the last competition. He didn't qualify for the finals. I'm not sure if it's the pain he's evidently in, or the pain pills he's taking for it."

Jeremy gave a slight nod. He began to wonder how long his dad had lived with the pain. "Do you think that's why he was so opposed to me competing against him?"

Shep ran a comforting hand down Jeremy's back. "I reckon. Doesn't excuse what he did though."

"No, I know it doesn't." He shifted to look into Shep's understanding eyes. "Evidently retaining that belt buckle means more to him than I do. I'm not sure how to feel about that."

Shep kissed Jeremy's temple as he wrapped his arms around him. "No one can answer that but you." Shep sighed. "It's hard to explain to someone who hasn't been through it, but for a man like your dad winning is everything. Todd's not exceptionally smart, and he's actually pretty lazy as far as work goes. This. Riding. It's the only thing he knows how to do."

Jeremy suddenly felt pity for the man who'd not only broken his ribs, but punched him in the face as well. He dug into his soul for answers to the questions he was too embarrassed to voice.

When he'd first started to learn the art of bull riding, it was to get his dad's attention. He was a lonely kid whose mother worked all the time just to make ends meet. Watching his dad on television, Jeremy had made him into some kind of super hero. He just knew if he learned how to ride his dad would welcome him with open arms.

The death of his mother had come as a shock. He still mourned her passing in his own way. Although she hadn't shown him as much love or attention as he would've liked, she'd kept a roof over his head and food in his stomach.

With the death of his mother came Jeremy's chance to get to know his father. He'd spent hours studying his dad as he rode bulls every weekend. Waiting, training in secret, he'd yearned for the respect and approval his dad only seemed to show other cowboys. The memory of the subsequent fight and broken ribs tore through him as if it had just happened yesterday.

After that first attempt, he knew his dad's feelings on the matter, so why did he try again? Was he still looking for approval, or was he merely trying to get back at his dad? Why was it still so important to him?

He looked at Shep. He had all the happiness he'd ever need in the blue eyes in front of him. What in the world did he still have to prove? Nothing.

Standing, he brushed off the seat of his jeans and held out his hand. "Come on. Let's go home."

Shep looked up at him with a shocked expression on his beautiful face. "Huh?"

Jeremy tugged on Shep's hand until his lover finally stood. "What we have together is so much more than anything Dad will probably be capable of. This may be his last moment in the limelight, and I think I'll let him have it."

Shep pulled Jeremy into his arms and kissed him. "I couldn't be more proud of you than I am at this moment. I love you."

Jeremy scraped his teeth across Shep's jaw. "Let's go inform the officials. Maybe there's time for them to get hold of Logan. It might just be the guy's lucky day."

Chapter Fourteen

After a leisurely day spent in bed, Shep was actually looking forward to the dance. He didn't do it often, and he'd never done it with Jeremy, but holding his lover close on the dance floor sounded like heaven.

Jeremy had disappeared after their pleasurable shower, to go back to the bunkhouse to change. Shep tossed his favourite royal blue snap front shirt and a pair of black jeans onto the bed, before taking a seat beside them. He needed to talk to Jeremy about moving in permanently, after all, he'd planted a tree for the guy. He smiled. Life was good.

"You ready?" Jeremy called up the stairs.

Shep looked down at his still nude body and ran a hand over his half-hard cock. "Not quite." He chuckled when he heard his lover running up the steps.

Jeremy walked into the room and whistled. "Well, well, well. Looks like I got here just in time."

Shep leaned back on the bed, resting on his forearms. "You gonna help me...dress?"

Jeremy shook his head no and knelt between Shep's spread thighs. Without a word, he swallowed the length of Shep's cock. Damn his cowboy was good.

* * * *

By the time they finally made it to town, the street dance was in full swing. Jeremy waved to Nate and Rio. "Where's Ryan?" he asked, stepping up to the two men.

Nate rolled his eyes. "Trying to break up a fight between Logan and Jax. Ryan wasn't in the greatest of moods, so I imagine the two will end up in the town's only jail cell."

Shep chuckled beside him. "How'd Logan do in the rodeo? Did they get in touch with him in time?"

"Yeah," Nate shook his head. "The guy should've kept his ass at home though. He got knocked unconscious before even getting out of the gate. He was on top of that mean sonofabitch Tabasco Red you all bred. Red bucked while in the chute and Logan flew forward, knocking heads with the monster."

"Shit," Jeremy said. "I guess if he's well enough to get into a fight with Jax, he wasn't hurt too bad."

Nate chuckled. "I imagine that's what the two of them are fighting over. Doc treated and released Logan, but he gave him strict orders to go home and get some rest." Nate looked at the crowd around them. "It appears he's yet to make it there."

The current song ended and a two-step started. Jeremy looked at Shep. "If you guys will excuse us, Shep's promised me a stroll around the dance floor."

Rio looked down at Shep's knee still in the brace. "I can see you'll be a graceful pair to watch," he laughed.

"Doesn't matter," Jeremy said, pulling Shep towards the band. "The important thing is to be in your arms," he said to Shep.

Shep kissed Jeremy's neck. "Someday we'll go out and do it properly, but for now, you'll probably have to settle for being held."

"That'll never be settling," Jeremy informed him, as Shep spun him around and into his strong arms. He ran his fingers through the hair at the nape of Shep's neck, totally content to sway to the music.

"After we get up in the morning, I thought maybe we'd get your stuff moved over to the house," Shep said in his ear.

Jeremy grinned to himself before pulling back and looking into Shep's eyes. "I was wondering when you'd get around to asking. Bo gives me shit about it every time I go back to change."

"Speaking of," Shep grumbled.

A tap to his shoulder had Jeremy turning to find Bo. "Hey," he greeted his friend.

"I thought Rance was coming, but I can't find him. You guys seen him?"

Jeremy shook his head. "Sorry."

"If he's here, he'll be well away from the crowds, you can bet on that," Shep replied. "Now, if you don't mind, I'm trying to romance my date."

Laughing, Bo waved and left.

Jeremy was proud of Shep as his lover lasted another two songs. "Okay, my knee's officially starting to throb. Can we find a couple of chairs and have a beer?" Shep asked.

"Sure," Jeremy gave Shep a deep kiss before leading his injured man from the large dance floor that had been set up at one end of Main Street.

They walked to the beer garden and Jeremy had to dig out his ID to show Mr. Brewster who was manning the entrance. Shep pointed towards an empty table. "I'm gonna go sit." He gave Jeremy a wad of bills. "Why don't you just get us a pitcher. I'm feeling mighty thirsty."

Stepping up to the makeshift bar, Jeremy ordered a pitcher of beer and an extra large iced tea for himself. From the sounds of it, his partner was about to get shitfaced and one of them had to drive home.

He managed to weave his way through the crowded area without spilling a drop. Plunking the pitcher down on the table, he took the plastic cup from his teeth and poured Shep a beer. Taking a seat he sipped at his tea and looked around. What a great town, he thought. Everyone seemed to be having the time of their life.

Pointing towards the stage, Jeremy leaned forward. "Look who's on the make."

Shep looked over and whistled.

There was Regina, practically throwing her exposed breasts in Trick Allen's face. Jeremy couldn't help but to notice the way the singer's eyes kept travelling from Regina to George Manning, the local fire chief. He'd heard the two of them had grown up together. George had been the one responsible for luring Trick and his band to town. He wondered...the way the two men looked at each other was more than friendly. Nah. Trick's sexual escapades were almost legendary. Nope, Regina was a lot more Trick's style from everything he'd seen in the magazines.

Several friends stopped by the table and sat long enough to drink a beer, but it must've been obvious to most of them that he and Shep were content on their own. Shep was well into his second pitcher, when Jeremy spotted his dad walking towards him.

Once again, Todd was surrounded by women on the make. Rance had informed them when he stopped by earlier that Cattle Valley Deputy Rick Buchanon had surprised everyone by barely edging out Todd for first place.

As Jeremy watched his father walk towards them, he could see the awkward way in which his dad moved. It was almost like every step was painful and suddenly Jeremy felt nothing but pure pity for his dad.

Todd stepped up to the table and pushed his large straw hat back on his head. "So, chickened out, did ya?"

He felt Shep's hand squeeze his thigh under the table. No doubt his lover was waiting for Jeremy to rub his withdrawal in his dad's face. But he couldn't do it. "I don't want to compete with you, Dad. I just wanted to earn your respect, but it dawned on me that nothing I did would ever earn me that."

Todd started to say something, but snapped his jaw shut. Jeremy watched as his dad's Adam's apple bobbed several times as the man swallowed. And then it happened. Jeremy's eyes locked with his father's, and in the space of a minute his dad must've seen the truth of what Jeremy had done for him.

Todd blinked several times. He leaned forward, putting his mouth close to Jeremy's ear. "You did it today, Son." His dad stood and nodded to Shep. "Make him happy, or I'll track you down."

"We'll be at the ranch if you're ever in need," Shep replied.

Todd gave them a half-smile before turning back to his adoring fans.

After his dad left, Shep put an arm around Jeremy and pulled him into a kiss. He could taste the hops and barley on his lover's tongue as they played tonsil hockey right there in the centre of town.

When Shep pulled back, he smiled. "You're a bigger man than I am. I think I'd have given him what for."

Jeremy shrugged. "He's already paying for his sins, and I have a feeling it'll only get worse. He took me in when I lost my mom and introduced me to you. How could I ever truly hate a man who did those things?"

Shep finished off his beer and stood. "Come on, cowboy. Take this ex-rodeo bum home and remind him how lucky he is."

"I'll happily remind you every day of our lives."

About the Author

An avid reader for years, one day Carol Lynne decided to write her own brand of erotic romance. Carol juggles between being a full-time mother and a full-time writer. These days, you can usually find Carol either cleaning jelly out of the carpet or nestled in her favourite chair writing steamy love scenes.

Carol loves to hear from readers. You can find her contact information, website details and author profile page at http://www.total-e-bound.com

Total-E-Bound Publishing

www.total-e-bound.com

Take a look at our exciting range of literagasmic™
erotic romance titles and discover pure quality
at Total-E-Bound.

Made in the USA
Middletown, DE
07 May 2023

30173077R00156